English Carols
and SCOTTISH
BAGPIPES

English Carols
and SCOTTISH BAGPIPES

Two Victorian Romances
Ignite New Holiday Traditions

Pamela Griffin
Jill Stengl

BARBOUR
PUBLISHING

© 2006 *I Saw Three Ships* by Pamela Griffin
© 2006 *A Right, Proper Christmas* by Jill Stengl

ISBN 1-59789-349-8

Cover image by Getty Images
Photographer: Will & Deni McIntyre
Illustrations:
    Ship by Mari Goering
    Kittens by Anne Elisabeth Stengl

All scripture quotations are taken from the King James Version of the Bible.

Published by Barbour Publishing, Inc., P.O. Box 719, Uhrichsville, Ohio 44683, www.barbourbooks.com

Our mission is to publish and distribute inspirational products offering exceptional value and biblical encouragement to the masses.

ecpa Member of the
Evangelical Christian
Publishers Association

Printed in the United States of America.
5 4 3 2 1

I Saw Three Ships

by Pamela Griffin

Dedication

To my critique partners who helped on this project, a warm, heartfelt thank you, especially to Mom who is always there for me, and to my friends Adrie Ashford (O'Mooky) who gave so much of her time and herself to help me with this, and Jill Stengl who did likewise at a moment's notice. *Nollaig chridheil!* (Merry Christmas!)

Who can understand his errors?
cleanse thou me from secret faults.
PSALM 19:12

Chapter 1

Scotland, Mid-Nineteenth Century

With her gaze upon the ever-changing water, Rachel MacIvor sat on the heather-clad hill, aware of a peculiar insight that the pattern of her world would soon change. Yet she did not want her world to change. Once, years ago, perhaps. But not any longer.

She looked out over the simple fishing village, a gateway to the Highlands, near a wide stretch of river that bordered her home. Rose and gold filled the sky, casting a shimmering mantle of vibrant color upon the silvery-black water. The dark silhouette of her grandmother's croft could be seen from this vantage point, and as the colors in the sky slowly faded to twilight, Rachel pondered her weekly visit.

Seanmhair had been pensive this afternoon. Clearly something troubled her mind, as often as she'd glanced at Rachel while together they cleaned and prepared the fish. Normally one to inquire and not a bit apprehensive to speak her mind, Rachel refrained from asking the cause of her grandmother's odd behavior. Without understanding why, she realized that, should she ask, her grandmother's response might upset the everyday order of life as Rachel had come to prefer it. Often Seanmhair's aged blue eyes had turned toward the window that faced the Clyde, and Rachel would follow her gaze to see the graceful bow of a sailing vessel or a flock of birds sweeping over the water. Usually she enjoyed her visit to Seanmhair's, but today she'd felt no compunction about leaving before sunset. Now, however, the gloaming filled the heavens, and she knew a moment's guilt. That she'd sat on this hill and stared at the river for so long might cause concern if she were to return home late.

As she began to rise, a ship's silhouette came into view against the pink and violet sky. Before tonight she'd always looked away. But this evening she watched as the vessel sailed closer, and she recognized it as belonging to the small, family-owned Sinclair Shipwrights. Inadvertently, her eyes swept to the right to the turrets of the square stone dwelling that perched atop a distant outcropping of rock.

Malcolm.

Bittersweet memories filled the wayward corners of her heart. Rachel had heard he'd returned home two weeks past to attend his father's funeral, but she had yet to see him. Not that she desired to. Far from it. Her dreams were too grandiose, she'd been told, and likely that was true. But her aspirations were never small, and she still couldn't accept the loss. It seemed an eternity since the bitter week Malcolm left for university, something they'd both known he must do, but an action she'd always felt would be preceded by a farewell on his part. But there had been no farewell, no word of explanation as to why he should so abruptly take off without coming to see her. How could he have been so cruel? After all they'd been to one another, how could he just vanish like a nighttime wraith in the emergence of dawn?

Upset, Rachel stood and brushed off the back of her skirts. Gathering her wool plaid tightly about her shoulders before facing the stout wind, she turned her back to the river and the ship it contained. With her teeth clenched in resolution, she climbed the path toward her parents' cottage. She had dallied long enough, dwelling in fantasies. For the most part she'd put such absurd inventions of her mind far behind her, but each time she viewed a ship, she wondered—at one time in her life she had hoped. . .

She shook her head fiercely at the wayward thoughts that broke through the gate she'd long ago erected against them. She'd been a fool to think the son of a wealthy shipbuilder would aspire so low as to seek a permanent relationship with herself, a simple lass, and once nothing more than a shepherdess. That was how she'd met him, all those years ago.

Closing her mind to the memory, firmly shutting the gate upon it once more, she continued her course up the hill strewn with autumn's remnants of heather and milky-golden thistle. Her attention latched onto the silhouette of a man standing in the distant shadows of some pines. Likely it was her father or her brother, Dougal, coming to meet her. As she drew close, her breath stalled in shock and her mind took root in a quagmire of disbelief.

He walked toward her, his stride graceful. She could see by the breadth of his shoulders, the slenderness of his build, and the height of his stature that this dark-haired man was not her brother or father. The cut of his frock coat appeared costly. The angles of his face were as defined and perfect as she remembered them. Faint lines bracketed his nose, but they only served to make him more striking. His lips were slightly parted, as though he would speak, and for one unwelcome moment she remembered the feel of them against hers. She lifted her gaze to his eyes—as stormy green and mesmerizing as the river in turbulent weather—and steeled her heart against him.

"Rachel." The rich timbre of her name from his lips produced an unwanted shiver within her being.

"Malcolm." She said the greeting offhand, as if it had been only minutes since she'd last seen him and not years, though her quickened pulse belied her veneer of indifference. She grabbed both sides of her skirt and moved past in an effort to show that his existence mattered not one whit to her.

He fell into step beside her.

Neither of them spoke.

Rachel's recent thoughts of this man, of all that they'd been and could have been to one another, increased her ire. Her annoyance got the better of her and she whirled to face him. "Why have ye come?"

"I had t' see ye, t' speak with ye."

"Did ye now? And whatever for? I canna think why. Tae say good-bye, perhaps?"

He winced but did not respond.

His lack of an explanation served only to fuel her irritation. She thrust her palm against his shoulder, pushing him a step back. "You're an unfeeling rogue, Malcolm Sinclair, and that's all ye be, make no mistake aboot it." Another push with her other hand. "I'd hoped ye would drown in the river the day it took ye!"

After the third time she pushed him, he grabbed her upper arms to stop her. He leaned in close, their foreheads almost touching. "Still made up o' fire and spirit, I see. Yet could I expect any less from me wee Rachel?"

His low rolling words, the intense look in his eyes were almost her undoing—until he added the last.

She jerked her arms free of his hold and retreated a step before her traitorous senses could propel her to embrace him. "I am no' your wee Rachel. Nor shall I ever be. So I'll thank ye t' go back where ye came from and leave me alone!" Turning on her heel, she pivoted away from him.

♪ ♪ ♪

Malcolm watched Rachel go. The set of her slim shoulders warned him he should not persist, but he must speak with her before she learned the truth from another source. On hindsight, perhaps he should have let her parents divulge the news, but he was now bound by his words.

The moment he'd caught sight of her slight form and the way she walked with such assurance, the striking manner in which the rosy sky glanced off her saucy brown curls—as free and wild as the woman who'd laid claim to his heart years ago—he wondered how he could have left her. At the time he'd been easily convinced it was necessary, and fear of her rejection had been the driving force behind his decision. Now that he'd returned home to Farthay House, he knew it would require every bit of persuasion on his part to get her to listen to him, while the gist of the message would take a miracle for her to accept.

Blowing out a breath, he hurried after her. "Rachel, wait. Please listen t' me."

She whirled around. "Listen t' ye? Once, I would have desired nothing more than t' do that very thing. But three years have made me ears a wee bit deaf tae your words, Mr. Sinclair, and I can no longer hear ye!"

His lips thinned at her sarcastic retort. "Stop it. You're acting like a wee bairn."

"Och, 'tis a child I am now? Humph. If it's only insults ye be hurlin' me way, I'll have none o' that from the likes o' you."

He forced himself to remain calm, reminding himself that she had every reason to be angry. He was deserving of her attitude toward him and more. "My cause for talking with ye stems from a far different nature than the past. I have a matter that needs discussing; one that involves you."

"Do ye now?" She crossed her arms over her chest and surveyed him with aloof incredulity. "I canna think what ye'd have to say that would involve or interest me in the slightest."

"Enough, Rachel."

Her expression changed to one of somber detachment. "Why did ye leave without a word, Malcolm, without so much as a good-bye?"

He tensed. Confessions were not compatible with her frame of mind, nor was he ready to speak them. He had hoped never to have to admit his faults to her, sure that the truth would only stir hatred, which she now seemed to possess in abundance toward him. Yet disclosure was imminent, though now was clearly not the time. Not if he hoped to gain her assistance, unwilling though it may be.

Her brow perched at a lofty angle. "Will ye no' answer me? Do I no' deserve even the favor of a reply?"

"Now is no' the time t' speak o' the past."

A disbelieving laugh escaped her throat. "Me most profound apologies; ye are quite correct. Perhaps we should allow another three years t' elapse before we do so." She gritted her teeth, let out a low growl, and started to stomp away again, but Malcolm grabbed her arm to stop her hurried flight.

"I'll thank ye t' let go o' me arm," she clipped.

"No' 'til ye cease with your tomfoolery and listen tae what I have t' say."

She tried to shrug out of his hold, but he tightened it. After another vain attempt, her mouth firmed, and she assessed him, her chin held high. "Bein' as I appear t' have little choice in the matter, then say your piece and be quick aboot it, so I can be on me way."

He'd forgotten what a little spitfire she could be, but this roundabout was getting them nowhere. He released her arm, striving for peace. "Rachel, I am sorry."

"And so ye should be."

He inhaled deeply and let out the breath through his teeth. "Aye, ye are right t' place any scurrilous name on me that ye see fit, but for now ye must listen tae what I have t' say." Before he could speak, a girl's cry sailed to them from the craggy slope.

"Rachel!"

They both turned to watch her ten-year-old sister,

Abigail, scramble down rocks to the path on which they stood. "Is it true?" Panting, she threw Rachel an uncertain glance. "Are ye really leavin' us and goin' tae live at Farthay House? With himself?" Abigail threw an apprehensive glance in his direction.

Rachel whipped her shocked gaze to Malcolm's and he felt the situation crumble beneath his feet.

"Explain yerself, Mr. Sinclair."

Her words came as frosty as the air that would soon sweep over the land with winter's approach. At that moment, Malcolm would have far preferred to face three long months of old man winter's frigidity than three more minutes of Rachel's icy wrath.

Chapter 2

Rachel crossed her arms over her chest and waited. Abigail also looked his way, and Malcolm pointedly glanced at the small lass and then at Rachel.

"Abbie, run along home noo. I'll be there shortly." Rachel relented, not for the sake of the cad before her, but because she didn't want little ears to burn with what she might hurl Malcolm's way should his explanation prove unsatisfactory, as she expected it would. The set of his broad shoulders, the telling clench of his smooth jaw, and the disquiet in his eyes verified she would loathe what was coming.

Abigail looked back and forth between them. "You'll no' be goin' with him, will ye, Rachel?"

Her features relaxed as she glanced at her sister. "Nae, wee lambkin. I'll be returnin' home soon."

Reassured, Abigail skipped off.

Rachel firmed her features into stone before facing Malcolm again. "Well?"

"Ye'll have heard about me father's passing, I take it?"

A modicum of remorse riddled her conscience, though she knew he had never shared close ties with his stern father; nor had she liked the man for his treatment of Malcolm and others he considered beneath him, namely those who worked for him at the shipyard. Still, decorum demanded she respond in a polite manner.

"Me condolences t' ye and yer *màthair*," she mumbled.

"Thank you."

Decorum was never her strong suit. "So oot with it then. Why have ye come t' find me? And what did Abbie mean by askin' if I was tae go with ye?"

He shook his head slightly, though she saw his mouth twitch. "Ah, Rachel. Your compassion overwhelms me."

His light words and expression carved her waning ire to another sharp point. "Are ye laughin' at me, Mr. Sinclair?"

"Nae, Rachel, never that." He sobered. "Lest ye lambaste me further, I shall speak. I am the new laird o'

Farthay House, as ye no doubt realize. Your father has given consent for ye t' come live there. Your presence is sorely needed."

"Me presence is needed," she intoned dumbly, struck by his words.

"Me mither has been ailing since me father's death. Upon me arrival tae Farthay House I found her in a sad state o' despair, and I feel a companion would prove beneficial for her. I spoke with your father and he has agreed."

Rachel blinked, standing as still and forsaken as a castle ruin. As the meaning of his words became clearer, she clenched her hands at her sides. Not only had his years in Glasgow evidently honed him into a pompous *eejit*, they had sapped him of all boyhood kindliness.

"D'ye mean t' tell me, Malcolm Sinclair, that ye've sought me out tae be a servant t' ye?" She could scarcely believe what her ears were telling her. After all they'd been to each other, after the closeness they'd shared. . . "After all these years, ye have the audacity t' stand there in yer fine suit o' clothes and order me tae Farthay House like some, some—mindless ninny who awaits her master's beck and call?"

Tears stung her eyes, and she blinked them back. She would not let him see her cry. "Aye, perhaps me *athair* works at yer shipbuilding company, Mr. Sinclair, and as such is beholden t' ye. But no one—least of all ye—manages me!" Despite her best efforts a tear escaped her lashes, and she swiped it away.

"Rachel. . ."

He held out his hand to her, but his tender exclamation of her name sliced at what was left of her pride. She jerked away from him.

"Dinna touch me! I'll no' go tae Farthay House t' be yer slave, and if I never see ye in these hills again, it'll be too soon for me likin'!"

She spun on her heel and marched off in high dudgeon, thankful when he did not follow. Out of his presence, she allowed the bitter tears to run down her cheeks. Despite her best efforts to repress such idiocy, all these years a slight part of her had awaited his return, had hoped, had dreamed—and for what? To be treated as a common peasant by his high-and-loftiness? She could have tolerated and accepted his sudden disappearance those three years ago if he'd been knocked unconscious and shanghaied on a ship to China. That she could have forgiven. Instead, he'd withheld any reason whatsoever for his disappearance. And then he'd had the unmitigated gall to order her to Farthay House, like some incompetent, newly hired servant who had shirked her duties.

An obnoxious, unfeeling ne'er-do-well! That was Malcolm Sinclair.

The view on the walk to her parents' croft was awe-inspiring; the distant mountains, craggy and snow topped, bore thick forests near their bases, and the quiet glen and low hills rolled like waves of a grassy sea. The peace usually found here was absent this evening, however. She could have been walking on blazing hot sand in a barren desert, such as she'd read about in storybooks, and not have known the difference.

Once Rachel opened the door to the cottage, her mother turned from the peat fire where she stirred something in a kettle for the evening meal. Rachel's brother, Dougal, sat on a chair and lowered the paper he'd been reading. Though none of them were educated by tutors or in a public institution such as some of the finer cities had, her mother had insisted all the MacIvor children be taught to read. A skill few in the village possessed. Rachel never told her parents, but Malcolm was the first to teach her the written language; he'd sometimes shared with her words from his storybooks as they sat on the hills for the few hours they'd stolen together each day.

Rachel grimaced at the path her traitorous mind

took and forced it to the moment at hand. The aroma of finnan haddock and bashed neeps, the smoked fish and mashed turnips of which she was so fond, tantalized her senses. But the look of anticipation in her father's blue eyes conflicted with the expression of dread clouding Abigail's small features, making Rachel want to retrace her steps out the door.

"Well, lass, did ye meet with Mr. Sinclair?"

"I did."

"Good, good." With a smile, her father rubbed his large hands together. "And did he be tellin' ye of the arrangement and yer new position?"

"He told me."

"Excellent!" He turned to look at her mother. "As this will be our daughter's last evenin' at our table, I'm thinkin' I should bring out the pipes and have a wee bit o' music after the meal."

"That would be welcome," her mother said. "And I have made all her favorites."

"I willna be going." Rachel's quiet words shattered the celebratory mood.

"What's this?" Her father's red brows drew downward. "Of course ye shall go. The opportunity tae live at Farthay House will be befittin' t' ye, as it will for all of us."

"Tae be a servant t' the great Master Sinclair?" Rachel spit out the words. "Bah! I want naught t' do with the man or with his màthair. I would be a scullery maid in an Englishman's castle before I work for the likes o' him."

"Hold yer tongue, daughter!" Her father raised his voice. "Ye speak aboot the family tae whom we're indebted. If no' for the salary the Sinclairs pay, ye would no' be wearin' such a fine dress and would have no time to while away in the hills as ye so often do. If no' for Abbie takin' over the task, likely ye would still be a shepherdess there!"

"I'm thinkin' it be pride and stubbornness that guides oor daughter's tongue, Mr. MacIvor." Her mother spoke with stern calm. "There is nothing petty or shameful in serving others, Rachel. Our good Laird orders us tae do so in His Holy Word. Yet yer fierce pride should cause ye great shame, *inghean*, for 'tis a sin indeed."

Rachel was saddened that her mother thought her a prideful daughter, though the ring of truth pealed in her words.

"Go off with ye tae yer room and think on what yer mither said, Rachel. And while ye're there pack what ye'll be takin' with ye tae Farthay House, for go, ye shall. We're beholden to Mr. Sinclair, and that's the way of it.

Now that he's taken his father's place in the business, I'll no' have ye be doin' anything to cause us shame or Mr. Sinclair displeasure."

"Aye, Athair."

As she walked toward the small back room she shared with Abigail, Rachel bowed her head with a tinge of remorse for causing her parents grief, though angry frustration ruled her next actions. She carted her battered valise from its corner, moved aside the curtain that shielded their sleeping quarters, and swung the valise onto the bottom cot with a fierce thump.

Had it been anyone but Malcolm who sought her services as his mother's companion, she would have gone, and gladly so. Yet she could not explain such things to her mother or father. Rachel and Malcolm's friendship had been secretive, likewise had their courtship, if one could call it that. A few stolen kisses—which she'd gladly returned—atop the heather-strewn hills far from the village and any seeing eyes.

Since the day eleven-year-old Malcolm had run across Rachel herding sheep, and her no more than nine years of age, they had become fast friends. Yet because of his strict father, who maintained no one of their social status should mix with the common, poorer folk, their friendship remained secret. Malcolm would meet

Rachel almost every day on the grassy hills, away from the severe dictates of Farthay House, and they would play and laugh. Sometimes they talked about their lives and dreams. Sometimes they read or sang Gaelic tunes together, learned from her grandparents. Always they enjoyed one another's companionship, until the day it grew into much more than that. As the years progressed and Rachel's father became employed at Sinclair Shipwrights, the need for secrecy became vital.

Half a year before Malcolm left for Glasgow, the summer Rachel turned sixteen, circumstances changed between them. No longer a shepherdess, since Abbie had grown into that task, Rachel nevertheless met Malcolm in the faraway hills. Often they strolled or rode on Malcolm's horse along a nearby lochan, staring out over its waters as they shared dreams, or visited the ancient ruins of a castle from the fourteenth century and the days of Robert the Bruce. On that day fire painted the evening sky as they watched the sun dip beyond the hills. They spoke of plans for the future, and Rachel put one hand to the crumbling wall of the stone castle, staring wistfully out over the lochan as she spoke. She had wanted her future to include Malcolm, though she'd not admitted such. Recalling that day, she could almost feel him draw near again.

"Rachel." Her name on his lips had been a breath, a query, a statement—laced with hope but set in determination.

With a queer sort of breathless anticipation, she'd turned his way. His fingers went to her chin, tilting it up. He'd stared into her eyes as if he'd never seen her before. A moment in eternity afterward, he'd leaned down and kissed her with such tenderness she thought the angels had bent low to the earth and swept her soul to heaven.

"Rachel?"

Dougal's voice at the door snapped her out of her musings. Embarrassed, she lowered her fingertips from her lips and jumped up from her mattress on which at some point she'd sunk.

"Aye?" Her voice came out sharper than she'd intended.

Dougal raised his eyebrows in amusement but limped forward, relying on the crutch he'd used ever since the accident three years ago when a racing wagon had struck him down as he walked along the road one rainy evening. "Ye looked as if ye were takin' a wee *spaidsear* with the fairies. Pleasant thoughts, I be takin' it?"

Rachel let her breath out in a rush. Taking a walk with the fairies indeed! "Was there a matter ye wish t' be discussin', Dougal, or did ye merely come tae torment me?" Though he was only ten months her junior, often he acted much younger.

"Torment ye? Me own sister?" The mischief sparking his blue eyes simmered down a notch. "They love ye, lass. Ye know that, do ye not?"

"Aye." The fire seeped from her but she couldn't resist remarking, "And I ken that Athair be fretful aboot his job and keepin' his new master's favor."

"Then ye ha' not heard?"

"Heard what?"

"Malcolm Sinclair promoted our athair t' the position o' manager. With a raise in salary t' boot."

"Manager?" Rachel's shock eased into disgusted resignation. No wonder her parents were nervous about Rachel causing possible offense. Malcolm had played his hand well. Father would now consider himself indebted to the new master of Farthay House for life. Rachel buried her ire, helpless to speak of how she really felt.

"Ye still have a yen for him, do ye not?"

"For who?"

"Who indeed!" Dougal scoffed but his words were gentle. "The new laird, himself, that's who."

Shock made Rachel stare before sputtering, "Why

should ye say such a thing? Noo who be *spaidsearachd* with the fairies? A load o' mischief ye'll be hatchin' if ye spread such lies aboot—"

"Nae." He shook his head. "Calm yerself, Rachel. It willna work. I sometimes would follow when ye met in the hills. I ken what went on betwixt the two of ye."

Speechless, Rachel sought for a reply but found none. She should have known her inquisitive brother would discover her secret; that he had carried it for so long and hadn't told anyone gave her surprise. Or had he? She sank back onto the bed.

As if reading her mind, he spoke. "Ye have naught t' fear. I willna tell a soul, nor have I done so."

Leery as to the reason why, Rachel idly snapped the buckle of the case up and down, studying it. "See that ye keep yer word, Dougal. Such admission could only cause harm noo. 'Twas a foolish infatuation and no more than that. I have no feelings tae spare for the high-and-mighty Malcolm Sinclair, I assure ye."

"Mmphm." Dougal sounded less than convinced. "Ye'll be going tae Farthay House then?"

Rachel released a resigned sigh and directed a look toward her brother. "What with Màthair and Athair practically bootin' me oot the door, how can I not?"

He smiled in gentle amusement. "I'll take ye in the

wagon. It's little else I have tae be doin' these days."

Despite her exasperation with him, Rachel's heart went out to her brother. Since the accident, he could no longer work at the docks, and spent his time whittling or helping around the cottage in whatever labor allowed him to sit or stand while holding a crutch. Yet he wanted no pity, and Rachel respected that, as she abhorred it as well.

"Fine, then," she agreed. "I'll be ready tae leave after me mornin' chores are done."

He turned to go, then halted and glanced over his shoulder. "And, Rachel, it might do ye a world o' good if ye whittle that huge chip on your shoulder, as well. It could drag ye doon should ye come across a bog, make no mistake aboot it."

Rachel just managed not to hurl her pillow at his back.

Chapter 3

Weary from perusing the shipyard ledger, Malcolm closed the huge leather portfolio. Except for the need for improving working conditions, which Malcolm mentally made note of when he'd toured Sinclair Shipwrights last week, he could see little else requiring immediate attention. His father had been meticulous regarding the business of shipbuilding, but when it came to the care of his employees Malcolm detected a laxness. Areas were unsafe, the men were forced to work long hours for little pay, and Malcolm sensed their discontent, though none dared speak to his face. Likely they decided he was his father's son and feared repercussions should they air their grievances. His father always maintained that the "underlings" he hired were paid on time and deserved no further consideration—an opinion Malcolm did not happen to share.

The sound of wagon wheels running over pebbled rocks of the drive brought his attention to the casement window. Abandoning his desk, he went toward the glass and pulled back the brocade curtain.

Rachel exited the wagon her brother drove, and he handed her down a satchel. Dougal then withdrew something from his pocket and placed it in her hand, at which point she reached up to hug him around the neck and kissed his cheek.

Relief and regret swept through Malcolm. Once, she'd kissed him in such a way during what seemed another lifetime. After last night, he'd assumed that the desired opportunity to renew their acquaintance had passed him by. Yet her presence at Farthay House must mean all was not lost.

His stride swift, he left the study and approached the foyer, where Mrs. MacDonell had just shown Rachel inside. He stood a moment and observed her. She stared, wide-eyed, at the high ceiling, the ornate walnut furniture, and the luxuriant tapestry rugs. It was her first time inside Farthay House, and Malcolm carefully watched expressions of pure awe and girlish delight cross her face—until she saw him. Her rosy lips closed, her elfin chin lifted, and her slim shoulders firmed.

"That will be all, Mrs. MacDonell," Malcolm addressed the housekeeper.

The elderly woman nodded once in her dignified manner. "Very good, sir. I'll just be readyin' the young miss's room then."

Once she left, Malcolm tugged on the ends of his suit coat to seek some measure of equanimity before approaching Rachel, who still bore the look of a Highland warrior princess ready to slay him where he stood.

"I am pleased t' see that ye've changed your mind aboot coming."

"I assure ye, Mr. Sinclair, 'twas by no decision made on me part." Her tone was as unruffled as the dawn's river waters but just as icy as yesterday. "No' that anyone bothered tae ask for me decision, mind ye, but there it is."

Her words pricked Malcolm's conscience. He should have handled the matter differently and given her the option to come rather than the order to appear. Now that he'd assumed the role as master of Farthay House, his attitude at times tended to reflect his position; yet he should have known better when addressing one such as Rachel and curbed his tongue. He had dealt with the matter unwisely, since his chief desire was to regain her friendship and all else lost between them.

Weeks of teeth-gritting silence and barbed retorts didn't appeal, and he decided to amend matters quickly. "I should no' have approached ye in such a manner as I did, Rachel, and for that ye have me most sincere apology. If ye choose t' leave, I'll no' be stoppin' ye."

She looked at him oddly, then gave a stiff nod. "I thank ye for that."

She turned to go, but before she could take more than a few steps toward the door, he spoke. "Still, upon remembering how much ye love a challenge, I would like tae offer a proposition."

She turned and eyed him warily. "Aye?"

"Stay and be a companion tae me mither for two months, 'til Christmastide. If ye find ye are pleased with the arrangement and life here at Farthay House, ye may consider your position a permanent one." She winced and he wondered what he'd said to cause such a reaction. He softened his tone. "If, however, ye wish nothin' more tae do with us, namely meself, you'll be free t' return to yer parents' home. And I'll never be darkenin' yer doorstep again."

She pondered his words. "And me athair—will me final decision have any bearing on his employment as yer new manager?"

Struck by her words, Malcolm studied the somber tilt of her mouth. She truly believed that of him? That he would be so cruel as to seek some form of petty vengeance? In retrospect, he deserved her misgivings. Nevertheless, her lack of trust in his character stung, much like his finger had when as a boy he'd accidentally sliced it on the blade of his grandfather's forbidden claymore. Rachel had shown by her words that areas of her life were now forbidden to him just as the sword had once been.

"I'll honor whatever decision ye make." He kept his tone formal. "Ye have me word on that."

She thought a moment, her gaze going everywhere else before looking at him. "Perhaps 'tis your màthair who should be makin' such a decision. We may no' be well-suited tae one another; she may prefer a more quiet and staid companion."

"Och, no, Rachel. She'll love ye. Of that I'm sure."

The words slipped out of their own accord. Her eyes opened wider in surprise.

Flustered by his blunder, he quickly sought to rectify the matter. "At present she lies abed."

"Is she ill?"

"Nae; lately she has little desire t' quit her bed of a morning."

He felt as uneasy as Rachel appeared. After almost admitting he still felt strongly about her—a fact that impressed itself upon him when he'd seen her the previous evening—now didn't seem like an appropriate time to offer a tour of the house.

Hearing Mrs. MacDonell's tread on the stairs, he felt a moment's relief. "I'll leave ye to yer own devices; I must return tae me bookwork. Feel free tae do as you wish 'til tea is served at four. We shall discuss your duties then."

A curt nod was the only parting acknowledgment she offered, but at least she gave him that much in return.

♪ ♪ ♪

Rachel followed the housekeeper to a sparsely furnished room more than half the size of her parents' cottage. She looked at the massive four-poster bed across from the huge fireplace, the wardrobe to the side, the looking glass near the wall, and turned to Mrs. MacDonell. "There must be some mistake."

"Mistake?"

"This canna be where I'm t' stay."

The housekeeper's dark eyes shone in disapproval, and her thin mouth grew even more pinched at the corners. " 'Tis no' tae yer likin?"

"Aye—I mean, nae. 'Tis a lovely room."

"His lairdship himself stressed ye were tae have this room. 'Tis the nicest in all o' Farthay House, next t' the family rooms, make nae mistake aboot it."

Rachel did not doubt the woman's words and pondered their meaning.

"Will ye be wantin' anything afore I go?"

"Nae." Rachel came out of her musings. "Thank ye." She felt at a loss. "Aye." At the housekeeper's raised brow, she hurried to explain, "Can ye tell me, exactly what it is I'm tae do here?"

"Do?"

Rachel gave a small shrug. "Am I tae wait in this room until Mrs. Sinclair summons me?"

"Is that what his lairdship be tellin' ye?"

Malcolm's new title sounded strange to her ears. "He didna say much o' anything at all."

"Och." Mrs. MacDonell eyed her thoughtfully. "Well, if ye dinna mind staying in this room the whole o' the afternoon, that ye may. Though if I were in yer place, I might take a walk on the grounds or in the garden. Last evenin' was a bad night for her ladyship, and I dinna expect she'll be makin' an appearance before dinner."

"Dinner!" Rachel could scarce believe a body could sleep so long. For the past nineteen years, ever since she was a wee bairn, she'd arisen with the first pink fingers of dawn. "Does she have many a bad night?"

"Aye. Since his lairdship passed on tae glory, it has only worsened, poor dear. Ye'll find that oot soon enough, I suppose." She moved closer as though about to unveil a secret. "She's from America ye ken, though her blood runs as Scot as the Clyde. Ye'll find she has some rather odd ways aboot her, though I'd give the life of me firstborn on her behalf, make no mistake aboot it. A finer woman, I've never known."

Mrs. MacDonell bustled out of the room, leaving Rachel to ponder her words.

Malcolm had spoken little of his family. During those carefree days when they'd escaped together to the hills beyond the village, they lived in their own fantasy world where reality was forgotten. But on those occasions when he'd mentioned his mother, his praises for her had been high, and for the first time, Rachel grew fretful that the woman might not approve of her.

She studied her image in the looking glass, trying to perceive what her new mistress would see. The dress her father called "fine" was so—in its day. Now grass stains from whiling away hours on the hills tainted the gray weave and braiding, and no amount of scrubbing had diminished them. Her *arisaidh* was worn thin in places, due no doubt to climbing rocky hills and snagging the long woolen plaid, and her face was too freckled for her liking. At least the faint brown dots—her penalty for enjoying sunshine and never wearing a bonnet—sprinkled only her nose and the apples of her cheeks. Strands of hair had worked loose from her braid, and she wrinkled her nose at her image. She looked like an unruly schoolgirl and little like a lady's companion. Despising the manner in which her hair was bound all around her head, she took out the pins and let her braid swing free, allowing the curling fronds to brush against her waist. If she had her way, she'd loose the entire mass from its thick plait.

With a sigh, she smoothed her skirts, took one last look around the room, wondering what to do, and decided to go exploring. She wished she'd dallied a tad longer at her parents' croft but had run out of excuses to delay her departure.

No one had given her directions, but she managed to find the garden. The sight of the cultivated flowers, among them red roses, made her breathe in the perfumed air deeply. A shaft of sunlight beamed through a broken section of wall, and she moved toward the puddle of gold that covered the stone path. Yet the light provided little warmth, and a chill she couldn't explain seeped into her bones. How long she'd been there before she sensed a presence, she didn't know, and she turned swiftly.

The shadow of a man stood in the entrance, and she sucked in a breath.

Malcolm?

The intruder to her privacy moved into the light, and she saw that it wasn't Malcolm, but a man with copper red hair and ruddy skin. His frame was muscular and stocky; he didn't appear the sort to tolerate sitting behind a desk, as was now Malcolm's lot.

"Well, and who might ye be?" His voice was deeper than Malcolm's, grittier sounding, but as he drew close, she saw that he and Malcolm shared the same gray-green eyes. Instantly she knew who addressed her.

"Ye must be Zachary, Malcolm's, er, Mr. Sinclair's brother."

"Aye. Ye did no' answer me question, lass. Who might ye be?"

"I am Rachel MacIvor, and I am tae be your màthair's new companion."

"Oh, 'tis that a fact noo?" He seemed surprised to hear the news, and Rachel wondered why Malcolm had not thought to share it. "I've been absent from Farthay House for some time or I might have known."

"Zachary. I heard ye were back."

Rachel turned at the sound of Malcolm's voice, noting he didn't seem happy to see his brother. His stance was rigid, his face a mask of displeasure.

"Aye, that I am." Zachary moved toward Malcolm, clapping him on the shoulder. Malcolm didn't return the gesture. "Like a tarnished coin, I am. Canna get rid o' me."

"We had expected ye last week. At father's funeral."

The mention made Zachary seem uncomfortable. He shifted his gaze away from Malcolm, then back again; his smile disappeared. "I couldna help the delay. I would have been here sooner if I were able."

Malcolm gave no response. Instead he looked toward Rachel. "I came t' tell ye that tea is served and t' escort ye t' the parlor." The look in his eyes bade no denial, and Rachel wasn't sure she wanted to refuse. Zachary dressed in fine clothes, but his manner made her uneasy, reminding her of a few dock workers who'd eyed her as she'd walked home from her grandmother's croft.

Perhaps it was all in her mind, but for the present, she put aside her ongoing battle with Malcolm and took his proffered arm.

♪ ♪ ♪

Tea was a strained affair. Malcolm had hoped to have

Rachel all to himself, not only to acquaint her with the running of Farthay House, but also in an attempt to rebuild their friendship. To his frustration, Zachary chose to join them and dominated the conversation. And Rachel.

She laughed at his brother's ridiculous jokes and listened with rapt attention to his unruly accounts of life at university. Following that, he regaled her with unlikely stories that took place after he'd dropped out of school last year, shocking the entire family, and engaged in traveling throughout Europe as a seafarer on a ship not Sinclair built. That, to their father, had been the greatest of Zachary's travesties, of which there were many.

When the last of the stout black tea was drained and the bannocks consisted of only a few crumbs on a platter, Malcolm hoped to draw Rachel aside privately for a few moments. But she was bushwhacked by Zachary, who'd learned she didn't yet know the layout of the house. Zachary offered his arm to take her on a tour, a tour that Malcolm had hoped to lead. With perturbed frustration, Malcolm watched his brother steal Rachel away.

Empty hours trailed past until dinnertime, though they were blessedly busy ones for Malcolm, steeped in bookwork. His mother remained absent, and when he inquired, he learned she'd developed another of her headaches. Small wonder, as much as she remained cloistered in her room.

A repeat of tea, dinner was a disappointment. Malcolm clenched his jaw, biting into his food with more fervor than necessary while listening to Zachary manipulate the conversation. At tea Rachel chose to ignore Malcolm, but now he noticed her dart curious glances his way. Once his brother wound down with his extensive version of his near single-handed capture of a humpback whale, Malcolm cleared his throat and spoke before he lost the opportunity.

"I trust that you're enjoying your stay at Farthay House, Miss MacIvor?" He noted that both Rachel and his brother eyed him strangely at his sudden change of topic. The words did sound trite upon hearing them spoken. He drained his glass. "Mither should be doon tomorrow; I ken she looks forward t' your meeting."

"Thank ye, Mr. Sinclair. The feeling is mutual."

Her uncharacteristic primness made Malcolm think he'd again wounded her feelings, perhaps by his formal address of her name, which he'd never used before. Yet he wasn't about to speak to her on familiar terms, not with his brother sitting there soaking up every word. Ever since they were lads, Zachary wanted what was

Malcolm's though he'd shunned his companionship. And though Rachel wasn't his, he had no doubt his erstwhile brother would try to seize Rachel's heart, too, if he learned Malcolm and Rachel once shared more than friendship—and that he again desired to share more than friendship.

Under his steady gaze that excluded all else in the room, Rachel's skin grew rosy and both she and Malcolm averted their eyes at the same time. He hoped his brother hadn't noticed and looked his way. Zachary busily cut into his mutton and forked the last bite into his mouth. Malcolm expelled a sigh of relief. His peace of mind was short-lived, however, when Zachary abruptly set down his utensils and asked Rachel for a walk in the moonlight.

She seemed flustered and darted a glance toward Malcolm, then to her plate, before looking at Zachary again. "I thank ye for the kind offer, but I am rather weary. 'Tis a long day I've had and I wish tae rise early so as t' meet your màthair." She stood.

"Of course, how thoughtless of me no' t' realize."

Zachary rose as if he would accompany her. Malcolm also rose, tossing his napkin to the table. She looked back and forth between the two men, surprise lifting her brows. Both brothers stared at one another as if they were rival contestants in a game of skill.

"Well then," she hesitated, "I'll be takin' me leave. Good night tae ye both."

"May I assist ye, Miss MacIvor?"

"She can find her own way upstairs, Zachary."

"I merely offered, in the event that she doesna yet ken the layout of the hoose."

"The staircase is directly outside the dining room," Malcolm argued. "Her room is at the end o' the wing. 'Tis no' difficult tae be finding."

"But unless Mrs. MacDonell has lit the lamps, the corridor will be dark."

"That's no' likely."

"Gentlemen," Rachel interrupted before Zachary could fling an opposing comeback, "I thank ye both." She smiled at Zachary. "Mr. Sinclair, your brother is correct in that I can find me own way t' the room I've been given, but I appreciate your concern as tae me welfare."

Zachary glowed under her praise, and Malcolm grunted. She turned to look at him. "Mr. Sinclair. . ." She paused, searching for words. Evidently finding none, she shook her head. "I have nothin' more t' say tae the likes o' ye. All that needs sayin'—on me part anyway—has been said." She gave a slight, dismissive shrug and left the room.

Malcolm watched her go, ignoring Zachary's smile at the manner in which she'd so thoroughly sliced Malcolm to ribbons. The lass needed no broadsword in her hand; had she fought for her clan against England during the Jacobite uprisings over a century ago, the enemy might have turned tail and run back to their lands at the lash of her words alone.

Chapter 4

Rachel undressed for bed then ducked out of the chill air of the drafty room and beneath the counterpane of the four-poster, somewhat bemused by the battle for her favor over dinner. With Malcolm, she felt angry amazement that he assumed he still had the privilege to win her preference; with Zachary, she felt uncertain of his motives, though she did enjoy his conversation and company. At tea and over dinner, she'd been more at ease in his presence with Malcolm nearby. But when Zachary offered a tour of the house, she'd almost declined. Still, she'd read no ill intent in his eyes and assumed she'd misjudged him in the garden. Sensing Malcolm's displeasure at the idea of her going with his brother, a rebellious imp prompted her to accept Zachary, and gladly.

If Rachel supposed things would settle down with the dawning of a new day, she was sadly mistaken. At breakfast Mrs. Sinclair made no appearance. Zachary and Malcolm continued the struggle for her attention, and after tea Zachary invited her for a stroll on the grounds while Malcolm offered an invitation to go riding. Malcolm's self-assured expression irked her. He knew his offer was difficult to refuse. Ever since the day he'd taught her to sit a horse, Rachel had loved riding with him along the sweeping terrain of barren moors and low hills that belonged to Glen Mell.

Disgusted with the men's childish behavior, Rachel declined each invitation and left the two brothers to share their own questionable company, opting for a book to read from the family library instead. It was there Malcolm found her minutes later.

She looked up from the first page of *Annals of the Parish*, which promised to be a pleasant book set in a small Ayrshire town, and eyed Malcolm with irritation.

She lifted her brows. "Ye wish tae speak with me, Mr. Sinclair?"

"I. . ." He hesitated. "Came t' get a book." He shifted his attention toward the bookshelves. Rachel returned to her reading, yet couldn't help but feel he was taking an inordinate length of time selecting one of the leather-bound volumes.

"How is your family?" he asked. "In good health I trust?"

She looked at him again. "Bein' as how ye just spoke with them two days past, I should think ye be knowin' the answer tae that question. Me parents are hale and fit, but I imagine me sister must be missing me presence somethin' fierce."

He flinched. "And your brother?"

"Dougal?" She shrugged. "He's well enough I suppose. He keeps in good spirits, though 'tis difficult for him since he can no longer do what he loves best. He helps around the croft and whittles his sticks, but I ken he be missin' the life he once had."

"He lost his job after the accident?"

"What man be keepin' a cripple for his crew? And what man be takin' one?"

Malcolm was quiet a moment. "Is he good?"

"Good?" She looked at him, uncertain of his meaning.

"At his whittling."

She thought of the gift of the wooden roe deer Dougal had given her yesterday upon their arrival to

Farthay House. "Aye." Her tone was soft. "He is that."

"What sort of figurines does he carve?"

With one hand, she slapped the book closed. "May I ask why ye're so interested in me brother's artistic diversions, Mr. Sinclair?"

He inhaled a deep breath and released it swiftly. "Me name is Malcolm, Rachel. Ye used it for seven years before I went t' Glasgow, since ye were a lass of nine and I was eleven."

"Aye, but the passage o' years changes things, as I'm sure I dinna need t' be tellin' ye. And it does no' seem proper for me tae be callin' ye by yer Christian name. Bein' as me athair works for ye—"

"It never stopped ye before."

"—and I'm in yer employ as well."

"When we're alone, as now, I canna see a problem in using informal address."

"And that is yer problem in a nutshell. Ye canna see."

His mouth thinned at the barb that went deeper than a mere discussion of names, and she knew he understood. Satisfied, she rose from the chair and tossed the book to the cushion. "I prefer tae leave things as they be," she said for good measure.

"How long do ye intend t' punish me, Rachel?"

"Why did ye no' say good-bye?" she shot back.

He shook his head. "I didna want t' hurt ye."

She blinked in incredulity and fisted her hands on her hips. "And what did ye think yer fool act would accomplish, *Mr. Sinclair*?" She stressed the name. "Me great and undying joy? Ye dinna ken what punishment is. I lived it for weeks after ye left for Glasgow without a word, and me no' knowin' for what purpose ye suddenly found meself unworthy tae speak with on the matter. But dinna concern yerself on me behalf. 'Twas soon over ye, I was, and thankful t' learn what an unfeelin' boor ye really be, before it was too late. I dinna feel a thing for ye any longer, make no mistake aboot it."

They stood staring at one another in a standoff, each unwilling to give an inch.

"Ahem." A woman cleared her throat from the doorway.

Both turned to look. Malcolm immediately moved in her direction. "Mither." He kissed her cheek. "How are ye feeling?"

"I heard voices in the library," she said in an American accent with a tinge of Scot's burr to it, "and had hoped to find my new companion. And here she is. Ye must be Rachel."

"Aye." Embarrassed to realize Malcolm's mother over-heard their tiff, Rachel felt her face warm as she moved forward. " 'Tis a pleasure tae meet ye, Mrs. Sinclair."

"What a bonnie lass ye are with all that thick hair and those lovely blue eyes; Malcolm, you were correct in your assessment. And with your gracious appraisal of her character, I'm certain we'll get along splendidly."

Surprise made Rachel dart a glance toward Malcolm, whose own face was suddenly as ruddy as hers must be.

"Aye, well, I'll leave ye two t' get acquainted then," he quickly muttered before leaving the room.

"Och, I seem t' have embarrassed me son. Though I havena clue why." She gave a soft wink, and in that instant Rachel knew they would become fast friends.

Mrs. Sinclair was a woman whose comeliness couldn't be doused even by her wearing of sober black widow's dress. With hair a fiery mix of red and gold to match the spark of mischief Rachel witnessed, and a porcelain sheen to her skin, Malcolm's mother took a person's breath away. Yet an air of fragility settled about her, and upon looking more closely Rachel could discern the shadows that ringed her green eyes.

She may have disliked the woman's husband for his cruelty, but not to speak would be a breach of etiquette. "I'm sorry for yer loss."

"Thank ye, dear child. He was a hard man, but I loved him." She shook off her melancholy. "We met on a ship, ye ken, one of his own, while my family was vacationing in Europe. But come. . . ." She steered Rachel back toward the chair, then took the one close to it. "Tell me about yourself and your family. How did ye meet my son?"

Rachel hesitated. Of course Mrs. Sinclair was ignorant in that regard, since neither she nor Malcolm told their families about their acquaintance. Neither did she wish to reveal the information now. Instead, she spoke of the small croft where she'd been born, and somehow the conversation drifted to the telling of her Highland ancestors who once lived farther north in the mountains, fierce warriors all of them. Mrs. Sinclair seemed not to notice that Rachel refrained from answering her last question, and when the housekeeper came to the door, diverting their attention, Rachel felt relieved that she'd successfully evaded the issue.

"Beggin' yer pardon, Mistress, but there's a man here tae see his lairdship on a matter of urgent business, and I canna find him."

"Very well, Mrs. MacDonell. Show him in."

The housekeeper darted a look toward Rachel. "Ye may wish tae see him privately, if ye wish tae see him at all. He's no' in a good temper; has a mouth on him, that one."

"Oh?" Mrs. Sinclair's brows drew closer together.

"Aye. Threatened t' bring doon the hoose, he did, if I didna fetch ye."

"I see."

Rachel stood. "I should be tendin' tae me own matters. That is—if it be all right that I leave ye." She hesitated. Just what was expected of a lady's companion? Perhaps she should wait to be dismissed.

Mrs. Sinclair gave a slight nod, her mind clearly on the matter at hand.

As Rachel left the library, she noticed a man standing near the outside door. He surveyed her with a look of superior detachment, though his grubby and ill-fitting clothes confirmed that he was as common as she.

"Are ye the blackguard's sister? If ye've coom tae send me on me way, I'll no' be budgin' from this stoop. Mr. Sinclair thought tae escape what he owed me, but I ken he's back hoom and I'll have what's mine!"

"Mr. Sinclair?" Rachel arched her brows in shock.

"Aye—the welsher owes me a fair amount for his gambling debts, and I've coom tae collect. He thinks his IOUs will keep him in good stead, but he'll no' pull the wool over Angus MacPhearson's eyes. I want what be coomin' tae me."

"Mr. MacPhearson!" The housekeeper's chill voice

rang with disapproval. She glanced at Rachel, then back at him. "Her ladyship'll be seein' ye noo."

A smug look on his face, as if he'd won a victory, the irate man followed Mrs. MacDonell into the library. He must not know Malcolm well to assume he had a sister, thinking Rachel was she. However, as Angus MacPhearson's claims settled in her mind, she wondered if perhaps she didn't know Malcolm as well as she'd thought, either.

She had known years ago that he'd taken to drink, as many men of the village did, though she'd never seen him in his cups; but to learn that he gambled stunned her. What other secrets had Malcolm hidden that she didn't know?

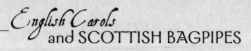

Malcolm gave Solomon free rein as the stallion galloped across the moors. His thoughts, as persistent as the stout wind, flew inside his mind. All of them swirled around Rachel.

He had known it would be difficult to win her favor. Yet his expectations had not included rivaling for her attention with his ne'er-do-well brother. With Zachary there to interfere in Malcolm's plans, the future didn't look as promising as it once might have. Malcolm had hoped eventually to regain Rachel's trust, to woo her, and one day, should the good Lord be willing, to marry his bonnie shepherdess. That was always how he'd pictured her. As his.

Malcolm approached a familiar area and thought of the day they'd first met here ten years ago. Then as now, Rachel's indomitable spirit had drawn him to her. He had been upset, angry, and fearful of his father, whom he never could please. After being victim to a tirade scorning his slovenly appearance and attitude, Malcolm escaped the echoing, bleak chambers of Farthay House to find solace in nature's friendly grandeur that painted the sunny hills of Glen Mell.

Wan and sickly as a lad of eleven, he'd panted as he ran and stumbled through the heather, engaging in a mindless race to escape something to which he was forever bound. Thistles scratched his legs below his knee-length breeches and tears clouded his eyes. And then he'd seen her.

When measured by society's dictates regarding comeliness, Rachel was no beauty like his mother. But she possessed an inner fire that made her glow and seem more alive than any person he'd known, even at her scant nine years of age. With a few black-faced sheep around her and a staff in one hand, she surveyed

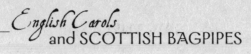

Malcolm as though he'd just crawled out of a bog. Her first words to him had been confrontational.

"Where did ye get sich silly-lookin' clothes?"

Malcolm had looked at his ruffled shirt, ribbon tie, and woolen breeches as if he'd forgotten what he wore, but hadn't seen anything silly about them.

"Ye look like one o' them rich, mutton-headed boys who canna wipe their own noses. Is that what ye be?"

Her taunts had made him angry, and he'd swiped the tears from his eyes with his sleeve. "I am Malcolm Sinclair, and me father is laird o' Farthay House," he'd said proudly, sure that this announcement would incite awed respect in her, as it had in the villagers who had dealings with his father. "One day, I shall be laird there, too."

"Och, noo doubt aboot it. Be off wi' ye then, tae yer grand home. I must tend me sheep." She'd promptly turned her back to him.

Shocked, he'd stared. Hadn't she heard him correctly? Didn't she understand who he was?

She turned all the way around to look at him again. "Are ye still here?"

"Aye." The answer came automatically.

"Then I'll be the one going."

Her saucy attitude made him temporarily forget his

own troubles. "Why must either of us go?"

"Me màthair says I maun have naught tae do wi' them tha' live at Farthay House."

"Why not?"

"The laird there is a scurvy and wicked king who eats lassies and laddies for breakfast." She growled the reply, holding her fingers out like claws as if to grab him when she walked closer. Suddenly she leaped forward; instinct made him jump back.

"Aye." Her expression was smug. "Ye are a mutton-head. 'Tis a wonder the king has no' eaten ye!"

"Am not." Her words had stung. "An' me athair is master there, but he's no king."

She'd glanced at the sheep in indecision, then at him. "I ken I could beat ye in a footrace, hands doon."

The very idea of a girl beating him in anything was enough to simmer his blood, and made the ancestral tenets of his boyish pride soar. He'd pulled off his jacket, his jaw clenching. "Tae what hill?"

She'd given a disbelieving laugh, but pointed toward a heather-clad hill some fifty yards away, then let her staff fall to the ground. After a final glance at him, she set off at a dash, her skirts flying and her braids bouncing on her shoulders.

"Hey! Ye canna do that!"

Malcolm sped after her, but even without her few seconds' lead, she would have beaten him by yards. She didn't gloat over the fact, which surprised him. Curious about her, and drawn to her even then, he sneaked out of the manor the following day, and again found her on the hill with the sheep. This time her manner had been more cordial. Within weeks, all aloofness disappeared and they became fast friends.

As the seasons passed, Malcolm lost his gawky boyishness by spending a few hours of almost every day on the hills with Rachel in the fresh air. His health rallied, while his muscles strengthened, and his body became fit and toned. Soon he was the victor in all their footraces and games of strength. As the years added age to their youth, so did it reduce their childhood tendencies, and they began looking upon one another as more than playmates. Malcolm was sixteen when he realized he wanted Rachel for his bride. And that had not changed.

Composed of courageous spirit and passionate fire, Rachel exasperated yet encouraged. She annoyed yet tantalized. Still, what others perceived as flaws, he saw as traits to be admired, even if she did drive him to the point of insanity at times. If not for her bullying persistence and her tendency to speak her mind, no matter the outcome, the milksop of a lad he'd been would have likely grown into a milksop of a man. Yet the one time her support mattered most, he had not trusted her ability to forget his failure. If she were to learn the truth of that night, she would always remember, and a dividing wall would spring up between them. That was what he'd told himself then, and his father's persuasions to mask the horrifying incident had seemed a godsend to Malcolm's tortured mind and anxious heart.

Yet what were these past years, if not living behind a wall of division separate from his Rachel? Would the torment have been so difficult to bear if he'd done the decent thing from the start and taken an old shepherd's advice instead of running away?

Malcolm brought Solomon to a walk as his thoughts wandered to Joseph, a mysterious hermit no one seemed to know much about. His gentle character and tendency to keep to himself caused the townsfolk no alarm, however, and as children, Malcolm and Rachel doubtless had been Joseph's closest companions, though the occasions they saw him were rare. Malcolm knew what Joseph would advise.

He would say that Malcolm must tell her, must ease this burden of guilt from his soul so he could again bear the sight of his face in the looking glass. At the same time, Malcolm didn't want to lose any chance of strengthening the weak limbs of his and Rachel's faltering relationship. Yet for love to bloom between them again, it must be nurtured with the healing waters of honesty. Only then could hope sprout and their love grow anew. Only then. . .

And yet, even knowing all this, Malcolm resisted.

Chapter 5

The days shortened and passed into a week. Winter's abrupt arrival caused evening's shadows to lengthen earlier in the day, and the frosts to increase.

Rachel settled into life at Farthay House as if she'd been born to it, and Mrs. Sinclair's company made Rachel's lot bearable. Malcolm's mother didn't treat Rachel as a servant, but as a friend, stating that if she'd wanted a servant she would have relied on Mrs. MacDonell to see to her needs. Long talks of her childhood and early marriage revealed the woman as considerate, sympathetic, and impetuous, and Rachel was thoroughly impressed with Mrs. Sinclair. Too bad her sons didn't share all the same qualities, though impetuosity did appear to be part of their character makeup.

Rachel's annoyance with Malcolm had waned but not entirely disappeared. She'd once been told that her temper was not unlike striking flint and steel against a tinderbox—sparking into an abrupt blaze to be replaced by a steady, smaller flame that could blow out as abruptly as it had been lit. Zachary, too, tested her patience, and she soon saw that the endless requests for her to accompany him on walks spurred from his desire to torment his brother. Rachel refrained from correcting Zachary's assumptions that Malcolm had any interest in her—other than as a servant, that is.

The Saturday after the week she'd arrived at Farthay House, she was surprised when Malcolm stepped into the parlor, where she was taking letters for Mrs. Sinclair. He looked at her, then at his mother.

"Have ye told her?"

"I thought I would let you do that." Mrs. Sinclair eyed Malcolm with a steady smile.

"Tell me what?" Rachel looked back and forth between them.

"We have discussed it and decided that your Sundays should be spent with your family," Malcolm explained. "I'll be takin' ye tae church tomorrow, and ye can go home with your family once services are over. Before sunset, I'll return for ye."

Flabbergasted, Rachel could find no words. She missed her family but never reckoned she would be granted leave to see them. When she only gaped at Malcolm, he gave an abrupt nod, seeming uneasy. "Well then. So that's settled." Without another word, he left the room.

The next day, Rachel kept quiet as he drove her to the village church.

"I am no' an ogre, ye ken," he said at last, breaking the silence. "I never intended for ye t' be strangers tae yer own family."

Rachel had no idea how to respond. "Then I'll be thankin' ye for that," she managed. The heat of her anger against him had sputtered to a low flame, and his thoughtfulness made it difficult to fan it to life again. Not that she was sure she wanted to. She still didn't understand what prevented Malcolm from satisfying her questions about his leaving, but these past days in his company kindled far sweeter memories. When he'd been absent, it was a fairly easy matter to push all such recollections aside; but seeing him every day forced those memories to resurface.

Ironically, the entire time she was at her parents'

home, all she could think about was Malcolm. When she almost buttered her smoked salmon instead of her bannock, she didn't miss the amusement dancing in Dougal's eyes, nor the lift of his brows that told her he knew exactly about whom she'd been thinking. She pointedly ignored him and answered the many questions aimed her way from the rest of the family about her life and the people at Farthay House. Thus, when Malcolm came to collect her that evening, she found herself eager to see him.

She said her good-byes to her family and accepted Malcolm's hand into the wagon. Soon the horse clopped along the rocky path to Farthay House while the dim moon made a crescent in the purple twilight.

"Is that King David?" she asked suddenly, speaking of the animal they'd ridden as children.

Malcolm swung his head her way. "Nae. Solomon is his offspring."

"And what of King David? Is he still alive?"

"Aye." Despite the shadows, she detected confused surprise on his face. "Tell me, why this sudden interest in horses, Rachel?"

"I would no' like t' think something happened t' King David. We had such good times, riding him along the moors." Rachel held her breath, waiting. By her admission she was letting Malcolm know she'd decided to bury the hatchet—and not in his head.

A smile lifted the corners of his mouth. "Then it is t' be a truce, Rachel?"

"Aye. If ye want tae be calling it that. A truce, Malcolm."

His smile lit up the dusky evening light. "More finer words I havena heard! I have missed ye, Rachel. Missed the moments we shared."

She almost ruined the present moment then by insisting on hearing why he refused to confide in her if he'd missed her so much. But she curbed her tongue before the question could spill from her mouth. Her mother would have been proud.

Malcolm let the reins go slack. The wagon took longer to reach Farthay House than their trip that morning, an obvious ploy on Malcolm's part to spend more time with her, but Rachel didn't mind.

Settling back against the hard seat, she listened as he recounted humorous moments of his university days. She couldn't help but note how his recollections differed from his brother's. Zachary's tales centered on himself, while Malcolm gave credit to others, sharing their admirable traits as well. After the telling of one prank against a professor, not instigated by him, or so he said, he let out a rich, deep throaty laugh, and Rachel's heart gave a tingling jump upon hearing it again. She hadn't realized until that moment just how much she'd missed his laugh. To her chagrin, her eyes grew moist at the thought of the years they'd lost and could have shared. Swiftly she turned her head to look at the water reflecting the colors of the sky.

"Rachel?" His tone was concerned.

Blast him, he always could read me well. " 'Tis nothing. A speck o' dust blew in me eye, I expect."

He grew quiet and she knew he'd discerned the true reason for her melancholy. Not until they approached Farthay House and the stable did he look at her again. He opened his mouth as if he would speak but remained silent.

"Aye?" she prodded.

His manner seemed intensely grave. "I wanted t' tell ye. . ." He hesitated. "That I enjoyed talking with ye tonight."

"As have I." Rachel sensed a peculiar awareness that this wasn't what he'd intended to say.

"And I should like very much tae go riding with ye tomorrow. If ye be willing."

Rachel's heart jumped, though outwardly she remained calm. "And yer màthair, what of her?"

"As I'm sure you've noticed, she prefers tae lie down in her room of an afternoon. Ye'll no' be missed."

To be with Malcolm again, to relive her idyllic dream of three years ago, was all she'd ever wanted. Yet she wasn't so foolish as to suppose she could return to the days of their youth. Such carefree times were behind them now. Still, if only to relive those days for one hour, for one cherished moment...

She couldn't resist the opportunity. At the same time, she promised her heart she wouldn't allow it the pleasure of trusting him again.

♪ ♪ ♪

The next morning couldn't pass quickly enough for Malcolm. He flew through the notices needing payment and upon seeing a familiar name, frowned at the retelling of his mother's meeting with Angus MacPhearson. That was a season in his life he wished to forget but a time he would always be forced to remember.

A movement at the door that stood ajar made him look up. He grimaced as his brother strode into the room and stopped in front of the desk. "A word with ye?"

Zachary's infringing gaze lowered to the strewn papers and then hit upon the open ledger. Malcolm swiftly gathered the missives into a pile, stuffed them between the pages, and closed the book. "Aye?" He set the quill in its holder and stopped the jar of ink.

"Mither wishes tae go to the village, and for me t' take her."

Malcolm's brows shot up at the surprising news. "And Rachel?" He could have bitten his tongue in half at his slip of her Christian name and the instant note of awareness in his brother's eyes.

"Mither wishes tae go alone to visit auld widow Lachlan."

Malcolm recognized the name of a fishwife in the village whose arthritic bones barely enabled her to continue her living. "Ye need me permission?" Malcolm didn't understand the reason for Zachary's visit.

An expression of disgust clouded Zachary's face. "I dinna need yer permission for any sich thing. I only thought tae mention it as we'll be takin' the horses."

"Leave Solomon."

Zachary looked surprised. "And take King David?"

"He's a sturdy horse."

"He should have been put oot t' pasture long ago."

"I'll no' argue the point with ye, Zachary. But for today, I need ye tae leave Solomon behind."

"Plannin' a ride?" Shrewdly he narrowed his gaze. "She is a bonnie lass."

"Leave her be, Zachary." Malcolm dropped all pretenses. "She's no' for you."

"Because she's under yer employ? Or because ye have a desire tae take her for yerself?"

Malcolm didn't respond, and Zachary gave a victorious laugh. "Aye, I thought so! Well, she doesna seem t' return yer regard, dear brother, and unless I see a ring circling her finger, I consider her fair game."

"She's no' 'game.'" Malcolm detested Zachary's coarse appraisal of the fairer sex. "And she's more woman than ye could ever handle."

Zachary seemed surprised at Malcolm's response. "Ye offer the challenge so boldly? Perhaps I should be takin' it an' no' look a gift horse in the mooth."

" 'Twas a warnin', no' a challenge, *dear brother*."

"Tae me they are one and the same. Or do ye fear the risk that I might win oor bet?"

"I dinna speak of a gamble. I am no longer a gambling man."

"Och. But I am."

Malcolm rose from his chair, his knuckled fists resting on each side of the ledger as he leaned his weight onto the desk. "Ye'll no' hurt Rachel, or ye'll have me t' contend with. Do I make meself clear?"

"I didna say I would hurt the lass. Only that I would

make her mine. By Christmas week, is that no' the bargain ye made with her? And ye no longer a betting man. 'Tis a shame."

Realizing Zachary knew about the private proposition he'd struck with Rachel, Malcolm opened his eyes wide.

"Servants have a way of talkin' when they think no one is aboot," Zachary explained, his manner nonchalant. "Take Solomon if ye must, but in the end I will have Rachel. And judgin' from what ye maun tell her, I canna say the same for you."

"What I maun tell her?" Malcolm was confused.

"As tae the wee matter of why ye left here so abruptly three years ago. And it does no' take a genius t' figure oot 'twas her that ye be leavin' behind." With a self-satisfied smirk, Zachary headed back to the door, leaving Malcolm in shock to stare after him, his blood running cold.

Chapter 6

Malcolm had been quiet ever since they'd left Farthay House. At first, Rachel was uncertain about riding with him when he'd explained they had only the one horse, and he was in the process of purchasing more. Yet the desire to share his company again, much like their childhood days, lured her to sit on the gray stallion in front of him. She had not reckoned being so close to Malcolm would again stir within her feelings she'd thought put to eternal rest. With relief she dismounted once they reached their destination, though she couldn't help but question why he would choose this place.

The castle ruins stood as forlorn as they had three years ago, facing the shimmering lochan that enclosed the gray stones of the abandoned fortress on three sides. The small lake appeared calm today, but Rachel wondered if untold mysteries seethed beneath its depths like the unspoken emotions that churned within her heart.

Her hand on the castle wall, she kept her expression placid and turned from looking out over the water to give him a sidelong glance. "Why did ye bring me here, Malcolm?"

"Do ye remember when last we were here?" He countered her question with another. "And what we discussed that day?"

His query probed the sensitive lining of her heart. How could she forget? And how could he be so un-feeling as to force the memory to resurface? " 'Twas years ago. I have forgotten much of that time." Her gaze went back out over the lake. She heard him draw close beside her.

"Have ye, Rachel?" His large hand went to her shoulder and he turned her around to face him. "I dinna believe ye."

The pull toward him now was as great as it had been then. Her breath caught. His smoky green eyes held the same promises they had on that last day they'd come to this place, when they shared dreams of the future and Malcolm led her to believe he wanted her to play a significant part in his. What a fool she'd been.

"I canna help what ye do or dinna believe," she said, not allowing herself to yield. " 'Tis yer choice tae believe as ye will. As it has always been yer choice t' do as ye like on numerous occasions. Ye are the master of Farthay House, after all, and need answer t' no one." She couldn't resist the small dig; she still smarted that he chose not to share with her his reasons for leaving.

He sighed, briefly shutting his eyes. "After last night, I thought we were beyond this. Can we no' leave the past behind us, Rachel?"

Rachel released a soft breath. His deliberate evasiveness irked her, but she, too, was weary of continuing down this bitter course she'd first chosen to travel with him. The flame of her anger had burned low and sputtered out. "Aye. Perhaps 'tis best."

She turned away, seeking stable ground for both her feet and her heart. Walking over the wild grasses, she pulled her plaid close about her as the chill wind bit through the weave, then she came to a sudden stop.

"Are ye cold?" Malcolm asked when she briskly rubbed her arm with one hand. The woolen dress did little to keep out the chill. Before she could answer, Rachel felt his cloak swathe her shoulders. The warmth of his body and his masculine scent permeated the fine woolen texture of the cloth, assailing her senses with shivering delight.

What are ye doin', Malcolm? What is yer purpose for all this? Why have ye crashed back into me life like a wave of the sea? Again the questions peaked inside her mind, begging release.

"Perhaps we should walk," she suggested. Trying to relive a moment from their childhood had been a mistake. Having him stand so near to her addled her brain. Christmas suddenly seemed far away, though it was a matter of weeks. She had agreed to remain at Farthay House until then, but she planned to stay no longer. And it would be wise for her foolish heart to bear in mind the folly of anything else.

His steady look gave her reason to believe he'd read her mind. He knew how much he was affecting her, and that frustrated her all the more. Not waiting for his reply, she began walking, eager to escape.

"Any faster, lass, and we'll be in a footrace," he called after her.

At the moment, that didn't sound like an objectionable idea.

"Rachel?"

"Aye, then a race it shall be, Malcolm Sinclair," she muttered under her breath. "Only this time ye willna turn oot the victor." She spoke of much more than footraces.

Pulling the edges of his cloak together with one hand, she took off at a sprint.

"Rachel?" Worried confusion riddled his tone, and she heard the grasses swish with his rapid footsteps behind her.

She ran faster, though she was no match for him and she knew it. Within seconds, he grabbed her arm to stop her and swung her around. "What foolishness is this?" His eyes opened in shock when he saw the moisture covering her cheeks. Swiftly, he pulled her into his arms and held her close, resting his chin atop her head. "Rachel."

Confused about her toppling emotions, even more confused as to why she had acted so childishly as to run from him, she allowed herself the brief respite of pressing her cheek against the warm linen covering his chest. His hand smoothed down her back. The wind whipped against them as they stood silent, sharing exultation in the feel of being held in one another's arms again, while lamenting the past that had kept them apart.

"I would have told ye, then, but I couldna do so," he said quietly.

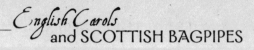

"Because of yer athair?"

"Aye. In part, 'twas due t' something he said."

She pulled slightly away. "Did ye tell him aboot us and he didna approve?"

"Nae. Though I would have told him soon." His smile was slight as he tenderly pushed back the hair blowing into her face. "But even then me athair's feelings on the matter could no' have kept me from ye, lass."

"Then what did, Malcolm? What caused ye t' run from me? Why should ye want t' run, when days before we'd shared such lovely dreams of a life together?" With all awkward pretenses behind them, the long-held questions burst forth in waves.

His expression sobered. "I didna run from ye, Rachel. Never think that."

"Then what?"

"One day, I'll tell ye, but today is no' that day."

"Why, Malcolm?"

He shook his head. Cradling her face between his large hands, he bent to kiss her brow, as one might do to placate a child. The touch of his lips on her skin did something unexpected to Rachel. Her heart gave a little jump, and she tilted her face upward as he moved away a fraction. His mouth parted in shock as he correctly read the unspoken message in her eyes. Tense seconds that rivaled an eternity elapsed as they stared at one another. Then, bending down once more, he covered her lips with his.

Warmth spiraled through Rachel, and she realized a part of her had been waiting for this since his return into her life. His lips moved over hers tenderly, slowly, as if rediscovering something very precious. When he pulled away, it was all she could do not to grasp his head and draw him back to her.

"I want t' begin afresh, Rachel," he said softly. "Tae start today as if the past didna exist and we had only just met."

She drew her brows together. "I ken that willna work."

"Nae?" His expression grew troubled.

"I would never kiss a stranger."

Malcolm laughed, the rich sound of his voice carried by the wind, and Rachel smiled at hearing it again. She would have to content herself that he'd promised to explain in the future his reasons for leaving, and let it go at that. He could be as stubborn as she, and it was useless trying to make him speak before he was ready. All arguments aside, she desired his companionship, and being with him today, like this, patched the hole that had been left in her heart three years ago.

♪ ♪ ♪

Over the next week, Malcolm and Rachel spent pleasant hours together, as often as their duties would allow. Twice Malcolm almost told her the truth, but each time she'd looked at him with a sweet, questioning smile when he'd begun to broach the subject. To see the trust again glimmer in her eyes, eyes that revealed the depth of her heart for him—an expression he never again thought to see—curbed his confession. He could not speak of treachery and deceit and duplicity when she looked at him in such a tender manner. He could not risk what he'd worked so hard to restore, only to have her heart turn bitter toward him again. At the same time, he knew the more time that passed, the more difficult it would become to tell her.

The sound of a step on the tiles shifted his attention to the study door. His mother walked inside.

"You're workin' late into the night," she said, her tone both curious and concerned.

Malcolm shrugged and tossed his quill pen to the desk. "I'm workin' on plans for improvements at the shipyard." He hesitated. "Of course such developments will require funds tae set them in motion, but unless we want a strike on oor hands, I see no other choice."

"I have nothing but the greatest faith in ye, Malcolm. And I know that your father approved of your business acumen."

Had his father known of Malcolm's plans to put the workers' needs above the demand for supply, Malcolm doubted he would have approved, but he smiled in gratitude and rose from his chair to approach his mother. "What are ye doin' up so late, Mither? Can ye no' sleep?"

"Och," she waved a hand dismissively. "Too many pastries before bedtime have made me quite restless. I am wide awake and have now come t' pester you."

He chuckled and took her arm, leading her to the fireplace and one of the chairs there.

Roses again bloomed in her cheeks where before they'd been sallow, and he knew that was partly due to the walks Rachel insisted his mother take with her. The subtle bullying to persuade his mother to go outdoors had worked well, and Malcolm was thankful he'd thought to acquire Rachel as her companion.

"I like her," his mother said, as though reading his mind. "And unless me eyes deceive me, you do, too."

Malcolm had no need to ask about whom she spoke. Nor was he surprised by his mother's straightforward manner; in many respects Rachel and she were a lot alike.

"Then I imagine it would be no surprise if I were tae

admit t' more than merely liking the lass, would it?"

"Not in the slightest." She leaned forward. "Do ye plan on taking it further is what I'm wantin' to know."

He laughed. "Mither, your subtlety is astounding."

"Humph. I never pretended t' be anything other than what I am. That is one reason yer father proposed to me."

"Aye, and an intelligent man he was. I canna imagine anyone dearer I'd rather have for me mither." He grinned boyishly.

"Posh! Enough of yer mollycoddling. I ken when you're trying to change the subject, and dinna think ye will succeed!"

He sobered. "In truth, I have thought much aboot the prospect, aye. Yet there is a matter which first must be addressed."

"You're talking in circles. To what matter do ye refer?"

He looked at her steadily. "The matter of three years ago."

The confusion etching her face gave way to understanding. "Malcolm Sinclair! Do ye mean to tell me she has no knowledge of what truly happened? That in all this time ye never told her?"

"I tried many times but it never seemed the proper time."

His mother let out an unladylike snort. "And will there ever be a 'proper time'?"

"What if Father had confessed sich a thing to you? Would ye have been so willin' tae forgive him?"

She thought a moment. "I would have been angered by his stupidity and actions, aye, but after my blood cooled I would have forgiven him." Concern returned to her eyes and she reached out to cover his hand with hers. "Son, ye canna keep such a thing from her. 'Twould be far worse if she were to hear from a stranger. The incident happened years ago, 'tis true, but someone might have seen or heard something that will one day slip out in conversation. Can ye risk having her learn the truth in such a manner?"

That was the fear Malcolm had carried with him every day since that night.

"Nae." He closed his eyes. "I ken I maun tell her. I will. Tomorrow."

" 'Tis best. And now I shall attempt to sleep again." She rose from her chair and Malcolm walked with her to the door. As he neared it, he heard footsteps hurrying around the corner.

He would have followed to see who'd been eaves-dropping, but before he could, his mother reached up to give a parting kiss to his cheek.

"It will work out, Malcolm. I'll pray that it does. And it would no' harm ye to do the same."

Malcolm gave a vague nod. His relationship with his Creator had suffered over the years, and it wasn't until university and speaking with a professor about the Savior that his life began to change. None of the Sinclair males had been praying men, and it was difficult for Malcolm to learn, though he knew his mother was right.

Only the power of God could repair this muddle that Malcolm had wrought with his foolish decision of bygone days. Had he listened to the advice of the shepherd Joseph, who surely would be considered a wise man had he lived in the time of Herod, Malcolm would not be struggling to fashion in his mind the words he must now tell Rachel.

Thinking of her fiery spirit, he winced. Tomorrow would prove whether his confession would aid in the restoration of their relationship or bring about its swift demise.

Chapter 7

The day dawned fresh with promise. Even the chill rain failed to dampen Rachel's spirits. She stood beside the parlor casement window and looked out over the sweep of waving grass that came to an abrupt halt beside the river.

Last night Malcolm had seemed distant, as though something plagued his mind, making Rachel wonder. After breakfast hours ago he mentioned his wish to discuss something of great import with her, and to meet him in the garden once his mother took her nap. Rachel assumed the reason he chose not to speak of the matter then was because Zachary had entered the room. But Malcolm's eyes had glimmered softly as he held her gaze before turning to go, so she felt the news couldn't be all bad, despite his grave countenance at the time.

Smiling, Rachel thought of these past weeks in Malcolm's company. Often she spied the boyishness still so much a part of Malcolm, while admiring the man he'd become. His arrogance at their initial reunion had departed, to be replaced by a gentle strength of character that attracted her. He no longer took to the drink, unlike his brother who imbibed a snifter of whiskey each evening. But Rachel hadn't seen a glass of liquor in Malcolm's hand since she'd arrived at Farthay House.

As time permitted, they rode together or took walks, reminiscing about their childhood while getting acquainted with the man and woman each of them had become. Twice in that time he'd kissed her, sending her heart careening into the sunset-laden clouds. But afterward he always drew away, distant, an expression of unease lining his brow. The manner in which he slipped his fingers midway into the pockets of his frock coat while staring out over the water with clenched jaw testified he was keeping something from her. He only answered her queries of what troubled him with a wan smile, and then changed the subject. She had never demanded he speak, but now felt that must be the matter of import he wished to discuss. At first, she toyed with the idea that his revelation might be of a personal matter, as in a proposal. Yet she didn't dwell on that possibility long, lest disappointment steal the wind from her sails should engagement not be the topic of conversation.

Eager to arrive ahead of him, Rachel made her way to the door leading to the garden where they were to meet. Hearing a tread, she turned expectantly, and masked her disappointment when she saw it was only Zachary. He came to a stop in front of her, a little too close for her liking. Still, she tried to be polite.

"Good afternoon, Mr. Sinclair."

His brow arched. "So formal. I should like ye t' call me by me Christian name, as I've heard ye use with me brother—Rachel."

His forward manner made her uneasy and she moved to sidestep him. His hand slapped the wall beside her head, blocking her escape. She looked up in shock.

"Noo then, dinna be impolite," he purred in a slimy voice. "I only wish tae spend with ye a wee bit o' the time ye spend with himself. Surely ye canna deny me the privilege. Ye might find ye even prefer me company."

"Mr. Sinclair," she said, stressing the words, "if I've given ye the wrong impression, then 'tis sorry I am, make no mistake aboot it. But ye are sorely mistaken if ye think I am the sort of girl who divides her time between brothers in the unsavory manner your tone suggests."

He let out an unpleasant, amused laugh. Rachel was distressed to see her earlier assessment of his character was correct. Yet she would not be bullied; moreover, from what she'd learned of Zachary these past weeks, the man was all bluff. She doubted, despite his bold words, that he would carry his actions further. At least, she hoped that was the case.

In one swift movement, she ducked under his arm while pushing him away with her other hand. He grabbed that hand.

"I'll thank ye tae let me go," she ordered.

"Why will ye no' go for a walk with me, Rachel?"

"I'm no' a fish or a duck." She referred to the pouring rain, trying for levity, though she failed to see humor in the situation. "Regardless, I wouldna care tae walk with ye in any case."

His lips compressed. "Because of me brother?"

"Aye, if ye must put a label on it, then there it is." She figured it best to let him know where she stood now before he took his infatuation with her any further.

He scowled. "And did he happen tae mention why he left so suddenly three years past? Did he tell ye how far he was in his cups the night yer brother was injured?"

His shocking words made her both keen to hear more and appalled to learn even the slightest bit of information in such a manner. To stand and listen felt like a betrayal of Malcolm, but she found she could not move, as if rooted to the spot.

He took her silence as affirmation to continue. "I speak the truth, lass, a truth he didna bother t' share with ye. I overheard me father and brother discussing the matter that night. Malcolm was gambling and drunk. Lost a fair amount o' money, he did, tae Mr. MacPhearson. He was upset an' driving the wagon fast, payin' no attention tae the road—nor the fact that he drove off of it and knocked yer brother doon. And then he drove away, leaving him lying there, bleeding and unconscious in the freezing rain."

Horror ripped through her heart. "They never found the driver! Yer athair suspected one of his workers ran doon Dougal. He even said so."

" 'Twas all a lie, Rachel. Our father didna want the scandal that was sure t' coom if Malcolm's folly was discovered; Father was having problems with his workers and didna want more. Malcolm would have gone tae jail, ye ken."

Her brain raced with what he told her though her mind felt sluggish, not wanting to absorb the revulsion of it all. Sensing someone draw near, she looked past Zachary.

Malcolm halted several feet away, his expression one of dread. But in that glance, she read the truth of Zachary's words. She walked around Zachary. Malcolm watched her approach, his expression wary.

"Tell me 'tis no' true, Malcolm." Her tone begged him to deny Zachary's claims, begged him to say that Zachary was only making this up because of jealousy. "Tell me ye didna leave me brother there tae die. The accident I could forgive, even the drinking and the gambling, but tell me ye didna run away like a coward an' leave me only brother t' lie wounded alongside the road. Tell me, an' I'll believe ye."

Sadness filled his eyes, making her want to scream. His jaw clenched, his face remained gravely calm. "I canna do so, lass, for 'twould be an even greater lie. And I'll no' be party tae a lie any longer. All that Zachary said is the truth of what happened that night."

Rachel blinked, wide-eyed and aghast. Instinctively her hand swung up and made sharp contact with his jaw. He winced, but showed no surprise.

"He almost died that night," she seethed. "If no' for Joseph findin' Dougal, he would have died! How could ye, Malcolm? Could ye no' at least have had the decency t' fetch aid? Ye almost killed me brother! An' then what? Ye ran off t' school and yer privileged life tae escape yer crime, while Dougal lost the job he loved and will always be a cripple because of yer stupidity and selfishness and cowardice." She shook her head, the truth of her bitter words making impact with her mind. Tears clouded her eyes as she stepped back from him. "I dinna know you. The Malcolm I loved never would have done such a despicable act. I—"

Angry dismay choking off her voice, Rachel hurried away, lest she break down in front of him. One thing was certain; promise or no, she would not stay at Farthay House another minute.

♪ ♪ ♪

"Malcolm, think before ye act. Was this no' your trouble before?"

His mother's concerned words stilled his actions a moment, but he merely shook his head and went on with the last of his packing. "I maun spend time at the shipyard, t' better understand the problems there. I plan tae acquaint meself with the workers, work alongside them—get me hands dirty for a change. One tour and reading the accounts in the ledger isna of great help when determining what improvements maun be made."

"Are ye certain that's the only reason you're leaving?"

His heart constricted with pain at the reminder of Rachel's absence. "It isna far, Mither." He turned toward her, resting his hands on her shoulders. "Zachary is here tae keep ye company. I'll no' be gone long." The bitterness toward his brother had waned, though Malcolm only blamed himself. Had he had the courage to speak of his folly sooner, things might have gone differently.

"You'll be back in time for Christmas?"

"I wouldna dream of spending the Yule away from me family."

"You'll take care of yourself?"

"Of course." He dropped a kiss onto her brow, then closed his satchel and picked it up.

"She'll come around, I'm sure of it."

Malcolm attempted a smile. "Of that, I'm no' so certain."

"You're not the same rowdy young man ye were then. You have matured—she's seen that. Give her time."

"Ah, Mither. I wish I had your faith."

"It begins by dropping to one's knees." Her eyes were loving but steady.

"Aye." With a vague smile, he left Farthay House on

foot. Since there was nowhere to stable Solomon near the shipyard, he had decided to walk the few miles.

Along the road, he approached a shepherd herding three sheep. Malcolm squinted in the late afternoon sun behind the man.

"Joseph?" he asked as he came abreast of the shepherd who didn't look as if he'd aged in the eight years since Malcolm had last seen him. His ash gray hair hung almost to shoulder level, and his beard matched his hair but was speckled with bits of remaining red. His face bore no more lines than before, and his strange eyes were as they'd always been—sparkling with merriment, while at the same time managing to be serene with gravity.

"Malcolm, 'tis a pleasure tae see ye. I had heard ye were back hoom. Is all well with ye?" His words rolled like the gentle lull of ocean waves, bringing to mind an angel's song. A strange comparison to the rugged man before him, but Malcolm couldn't help applying his boyhood thoughts to the shepherd.

"All is well."

"And how is Rachel?" Joseph countered. "No' such a wee lassie anymore, I'm thinkin'. Are matters well between ye?"

Malcolm eyed him sharply. Had Joseph looked into

his heart and found the truth written there? "If I were a drinking man, I would buy ye a whiskey and speak t' ye of me woes," he admitted, "but I frequent the pubs no longer."

Joseph nodded. "A good thing, too. Me home is over that rise. I havena had a visitor in a long while, but ye are welcome."

Surprised curiosity led Malcolm to accept. As far as he knew, no one had ever been to Joseph's home. Minutes later, Malcolm found himself sitting on the lone chair the humble one-room croft boasted. The sleeping cot was fastened to the wall and partitioned off with a clean tattered curtain. A simple but beautiful carved wooden cross hung on the wall above the table, and Joseph followed Malcolm's admiring gaze.

"Dougal made that for me a few months after his accident."

The reminder brought the stabbing pain back with a vengeance.

"Now, tell me lad." Joseph's voice was soft. "How can I help ye?"

Chapter 8

Since the day Rachel walked home in the pouring rain, threw open the door, and wordlessly hurried to her sleeping quarters—ignoring the shocked stares of her mother and siblings—her family was careful not to probe too deeply her reasons for leaving Farthay House. Thus it was with surprise that Rachel regarded Dougal as he hobbled to the table and demanded to know what was wrong and why she'd left.

She laid her quill over the list of items needed from the market for the densely fruit-laden black bun, sticky-toffee pudding, and other treats she would help Màthair prepare for the Yuletide. "Why should ye think something be the matter, Dougal?" she hedged.

"Because ye've been walkin' aboot like a wraith since

ye left Farthay House. A wraith with a look o' reckoning in her eye."

At least Abbie was in the hills with the sheep and their mother was outside so they couldn't hear. "I would rather no' speak of that place nor of the scoundrel who runs it."

Dougal's jaw firmed. "Did he harm ye in any way, lass?"

At the fierce protection that blazed in his eyes, she put a gentling hand on his sleeve. "Nae. No' of what ye speak. This goes back three years. Something he did that opened me eyes tae what a deceiving coward the master o' Farthay House truly is."

Dougal relaxed and nodded. "Then ye ken the truth o' what happened."

"What truth?"

"That Malcolm Sinclair was the unknown driver responsible for me accident."

Rachel stared in stunned disbelief. "Ye knew this?"

"Aye. I saw his face before he drove off that night."

"And ye told no one?" Rachel asked incredulously. "No' even me?"

"It wasna me place t' tell. What would have been the point? Once I remembered, he had already left for Glasgow. Since his return these few weeks past, I learned he is a changed man, no longer taken tae the drink, and he has plans tae benefit the workers, including our athair."

"Brought on by guilt, no doubt," she countered with a huff.

Dougal shrugged. "Whatever the cause, I do no' question. He came t' see me, t' speak with me two weeks ago. He apologized for injuring me and offered me a job."

"A job?" Rachel blinked. Dougal was full of surprises today.

"Aye. He said he could always use a good carpenter, one who can carve no' only well, but also creatively. He looked at me handiwork and liked what he saw. I start work at Sinclair Shipwrights after the New Year, when he hopes some o' the renovations have been made." His smile was bright. "I'm t' have me own wee office where I may sit and whittle tae me heart's content."

Rachel could scarcely take it all in. "But 'twas Malcolm who crippled ye and left ye tae die. How can ye forget that?"

Dougal pondered a moment. "I have no' admitted as much tae our parents, but 'twas a time when I took me own share o' the whiskey. Seanmhair was right tae call it the devil's brew. Too much, and a man forgets his own name. Such was the case with Mr. Sinclair that night. He and his athair had a row, and he went t' the pub tae get guttered. His mind went into a black fog. By the time he remembered the accident, Joseph had found me, and Malcolm's father convinced him all must be kept quiet. Shortly afterward, he sent him away tae Glasgow."

"If what ye say is true, why did he no' tell me?" Rachel countered.

"Did ye give him the chance?" Dougal's eyes glowed, but were steady. "Yer tongue can be as swift as a whip and flail a man at ten paces, make no mistake aboot it."

She arched her brow. "Was that supposed tae be funny?"

His smile was nothing but mischievous. "Simply observin' a fact."

She rose from her chair and grabbed her cloak, flinging it around her shoulders. "I maun go tae market before it closes and make me purchases, or there will be no black bun for yer Christmas." She considered. "No' that ye deserve any—make no mistake aboot that!" She finished tying the ribbons in a bow at her collar with a jerk.

His laugh still carried to her ears as she briskly closed the outside door behind her.

A light, wet snow was falling, but that didn't deter Rachel. She needed time alone to think about all Dougal had said. Once she arrived at the market, she knew she sounded scatterbrained as she read off the list of ingredients they would need. Mr. Watt boxed the items into a small crate. Rachel barely observed his curious farewell as she departed with her purchases.

Outside, she shook her head as she went over the facts again in her mind.

"Rachel, is that ye, lassie?"

Startled out of her reverie she turned to look behind her and instantly broke into a smile. "Joseph! How good it is t' see ye." She hadn't seen him since her brother's accident, and marveled that he hadn't changed from the time she'd first seen him when she and Malcolm had fallen into an argument while playing in the hills. Joseph had approached, putting an end to their spat with his calm words and habit of talking in parables. Since that day in their childhood, Rachel and Malcolm had seen him rarely, but each time the impact the gentle shepherd left on them was astounding.

"And how be ye, lass? Is all well with yer soul?" He reached for her crate.

Taken aback by the manner in which he'd phrased the question, Rachel allowed him to carry her purchases.

She craved counsel, and Joseph had always proven to be a worthy listener. Knowing this, she told him everything from the day Malcolm reappeared in her life until now.

They walked for some time before Joseph spoke. "The road t' complete forgiveness is often hard t' travel, lass. 'Tis filled with bogs that can suck a man doon, and briars that can scratch him. Yet for those who persist, the rewards be great."

Rachel threw him a sidelong glance, considering the wisdom of his words.

"Likewise if one refuses tae leave the fog o' the past, he can no' appreciate the clarity of the present life with which God has blessed him. A child thinks as a child, but maturity brings wisdom. There is a time when one must let go o' fantasies and embrace the truth."

"And ye think I live in the past?" Rachel asked.

"From what ye tell me, I ken ye do, but 'tis more than that." He halted on the road and she did likewise. "With Malcolm, ye both escaped tae an imaginary world as children. Ye came t' see him no' as the boy and the man he truly was, but as the person ye wanted t' see. Neither of ye spoke much aboot matters concerning ye; instead ye both lived in a world of escape."

"How do ye ken this?" She hadn't spoken such things to him.

"Malcolm told me."

"He spoke with you aboot me?" A quiver of tender amazement touched her heart.

"Aye; he was distraught, he was. But more distraught that he'd let ye doon and could no' be the man ye wanted, the man ye thought him to be afore he left for Glasgow."

"Perhaps he wasna then, but he has become such a man," Rachel mused.

"Still, he has failings."

"Aye, but he's trying t' amend his athair's wrongs and do what is right with his company. And he no longer takes tae the whiskey."

"So ye're saying there be worth in the man?"

Stunned to realize she'd been defending Malcolm, Rachel blinked and averted her gaze to the snow that began to coat the grasses. Dougal's earlier words, and now Joseph's quiet ones, forced a dark curtain to sweep from her mind. "Aye," she agreed softly. Despite his shameful actions concerning Dougal, despite his abrupt departure without saying good-bye—though now she understood his reasoning—her heart had never stopped loving him.

She grabbed the crate from Joseph's arms. "Forgive me, but I maun go; I have a matter that needs tending."

"Tae Farthay House?" Joseph asked before she could do more than turn around.

She again faced him. "Aye."

"He isna there, lass."

"No' there," she repeated, dread weighting her heart with a heavy millstone.

"Nae, nae, dinna look so forlorn," Joseph soothed. "He hasna left Glen Mell."

The stone fell away and a ray of light flickered. "Where has he gone?"

"I canna tell ye, lass. But when next ye see him, and ye will, of that I'm certain, let him be the first tae speak."

With a blithe parting smile, Joseph turned and walked away.

♪ ♪ ♪

Christmas arrived and hope birthed within Rachel that she would see Malcolm soon. While Abbie and Dougal hung boughs of holly around the croft, Rachel and her mother baked the black bun, the sweet puddings, and meat pastries of *bridies*. Seanmhair sat on a stool making her famous *cloutie* dumpling, and Athair was outside preparing the birch that would serve as the long-burning Yule log, stripping it of its leaves and bark.

Rachel sidled up to her grandmother. "Ye knew

Malcolm would come for me that last day I came t' see ye; that is why ye acted so oddly, isna that so?"

"Aye, lassie, I had heard of his plans in the village." She took Rachel's hand between her blue-veined ones. "I often spied ye goin' tae the hills when ye be children. Yer heart was then his, and still is, I ken."

"Aye." No longer surprised to find her secret was no secret after all, Rachel bent to kiss her grandmother's thin cheek.

Once the meal was ready, everyone ate to their heart's content, Dougal taking thirds. Rachel hoped that Margaret, a bonnie lass from the village, was expert at cooking, for she knew Dougal favored Margaret and she him, judging by the looks Rachel had seen the two share. A wedding was sure to be announced soon, since Dougal would again have income; and though Rachel was pleased he'd found a measure of happiness, she wished for her own portion.

Until recently, it had been unlawful for people to keep the Yule, due to an edict from the sixteenth century, but Rachel's mother had always insisted they observe Christmas since it was the day the Laird Jesus came to earth as a wee bairn. Prince Albert and Queen Victoria recently brought to Scotland new traditions, though Rachel's family kept a few of their own.

Athair brought out the pipes. Soon the lingering, soul-stirring notes reverberated through the croft. To Rachel's surprise, Dougal brought out their grandfather's fiddle that *Seanair* had bequeathed to him, but Dougal had not played since before the accident. When he first brought the bow across the strings the sound was discordant, but soon he played skillfully as he'd been taught by their seanair. Rachel noted the happy tears in her grandmother's eyes.

As the men played, the rest of the family sang songs of tradition. They played "*Taladh Chriosta*," "God Rest Ye Merry Gentlemen," and ended with a spirited chorus of "I Saw Three Ships." Abbie pulled a grudging Rachel up from the chair and linked elbows with her sister, forcing her to dance a jig.

"Then let us all rejoice amain,
On Christmas day, on Christmas day;
Then let us all rejoice amain,
On Christmas day in the morning.

"And all the souls on earth shall sing,
On Christmas day, on Christmas day
And all the souls on earth shall sing,
On Christmas day in the morning."

Dougal played the last verses faster and faster, and soon the two girls fell into a heap on the floor, dizzy and laughing.

"If ye could have it, what would ye wish tae be on those ships all three?" Abbie asked Rachel from where she sat on the floor.

Rachel looked into her little sister's merry blue eyes. She thought of the past weeks, and especially the last two without Malcolm by her side. "Peace, love, and forgiveness."

"Aye," her mother said softly from the corner. " 'Tis a worthy answer. Mr. MacIvor, I do believe oor daughter is growing up."

Chapter 9

New Year's Day brought with it another sprinkling of snow as the women engaged in *redding*, a thorough housecleaning, while Abbie took out the ashes from the coal fire in preparation for the Hogmanay celebration. Dougal regaled Abbie with tales of when he used to engage in the tradition of *firstfooting*, a custom wishing family and friends prosperity for the coming year. Always the first to beat his peers and race to the Sinclairs' door before midnight, Dougal arrived bearing simple gifts, while hoping the cook would give him a feast and a coin in return. He was never disappointed.

"But isna the first foot over the threshold supposed tae be bonnie, male, and dark?" Abbie wanted to know.

"No' bonnie, lambkin. Braw. And aye. So, I be two oot o' three," Dougal amended, and Abbie giggled, looking at his red hair.

"Why does no one come through oor door?" she wanted to know.

"Because we dinna live in the village," their mother was quick to explain.

"Why is that?"

"Because yer sheep prefer the hills," Dougal teased, lightly tweaking her nose.

She giggled and went back to helping stir the mixture for the pudding, satisfied with the reply. Rachel knew it was more than that. As was a common saying—"he's as bare as a birk on Yule e'en." The firstfooters, most of whom were young men like Dougal, desired a rich man's feast in return, not a poor man's supper, which was usually all the MacIvors could afford. Though this year, with her father's promotion and more bounty than they'd had on the table in years past, circumstances promised change.

They shared a leisurely meal late that night, as was their custom to see in the New Year. As the village bells began pealing, heralding midnight, Abbie hurried to the window to see.

"No one is oot there," she said sadly.

Rachel knelt to hug her sister. "Never ye mind. We can still celebrate, aye?"

Abbie gave a dejected nod and smile.

The sound of a step outside the door brought their attention to it, and Rachel watched wide-eyed as it opened.

A tall figure in a fine kilt and cloak stepped over the threshold, the view of a face obstructed by the many parcels he carried. The hair was definitely dark, he was most certainly male, and. . .

Rachel inhaled a swift breath as Malcolm's smoky green eyes met hers once he set the parcels on the table.

"Oh!" Abbie squealed in delight. "He's braw *and* dark—we're sure tae have good luck this year!"

"Shush, Abbie," their mother gently scolded.

Malcolm broke eye contact with Rachel, and, as was the custom, wordlessly set about adding coal to the fire from the mounds in the sack he'd brought with him. He stirred the embers to life, then rose to face her parents.

To Rachel's astonishment, he issued an apology, admitting his part in Dougal's accident and his cowardice in following his father's imprudent advice. Her parents blinked in astonishment. Dougal was the first to rise and hobble with his crutch over to Malcolm. He stuck out his hand. Malcolm gave it a hearty shake, then pulled him into a swift embrace.

This broke the solemnity of the moment and everyone talked at once, welcoming Malcolm with warm hugs or hearty backslapping as if he were a family member. Rachel glanced at the table, stunned to see *all* the desired gifts present, though many firstfooters brought few. But Malcolm had brought everything—coal, salt, shortcake, a sprig of greenery, a bag of coins, and other traditional symbols to bless them with warmth, light, and prosperity for the coming year.

"Rachel, a word with ye in private?" Malcolm looked to where she still knelt on the floor by the window. Her mother smiled in approval, and Seanmhair motioned with her head toward the door.

"Go on with ye," she urged. "We will prepare Mr. Sinclair a meal."

Rachel needed no persuasion. She slipped into her cloak and followed Malcolm outside, into the chill night.

"Rachel," he began, "I canna tell ye how sorry I am for all that happened betwixt us. Both in causing Dougal's accident and in keeping it from ye—"

She pressed her fingers to his lips to halt his words. " 'Tis in the past, Malcolm. What needed t' be said has been said. I hold no grudge toward ye any longer."

His eyes brightened with surprised hope. He circled her wrist with his hand, kissing the fingertips before he lowered them from his mouth so he could speak. He didn't, however, let go of her hand.

"Rachel, lass, ye are me heart and always have been."

Her own heart jumped at his words. "Malcolm, I ken I've loved ye all me life, but 'twas no' 'til Joseph spoke that I understood it."

He grew alert. "Ye spoke tae Joseph? When?"

"The day before Christmas. Why?" She was confused at the sudden change in topic.

"He's gone, Rachel."

"Gone?" She blinked.

"Aye. His croft doesna appear as if anyone ever lived in it. I went tae thank him for his counsel—he helped me regain footing with the Laird and also convinced me tae see ye again. All that remained was the cross Dougal carved, sitting in a ray of sunlight, it was. Joseph's croft is bare, as if the man, himself, never existed."

Rachel's eyes widened as she tried to take it all in.

"He did exist, did he no', Malcolm?"

"We both spoke tae him several times. He must have."

"Aye."

From inside, her father's pipes began the haunting tune "Auld Lang Syne."

"Rachel, me love. . ." Malcolm reached into his waistcoat and pulled out a stunning sapphire pendant. It shimmered in the light that the moon cast upon the snow. "This was me seanmhair's, given tae me t' give t' the woman I would one day take for me bride." Opening her hand, he laid the heirloom in her palm with care, then closed her fingers around it and held them.

Her mouth parted in shock at what she knew was coming, what she'd always wanted, but up until minutes ago, never dared dream could actually be.

"Would ye consider becomin' me wife, Rachel?"

Here was the question she'd anticipated for years, and she couldn't find her voice. She swallowed hard and searched for it. "Aye, Malcolm, I most definitely will."

His smile stretched wide. "Come here, me wee bonnie lass." He pulled her close and Rachel yielded, wrapping her arms beneath his cloak and around his waist. She laid her ear against his swiftly beating heart, reveling in his warmth and protection.

From inside, her family's voices sailed to them:

"Should auld acquaintance be forgot,

And never brought to mind?
Should auld acquaintaince be forgot,
And auld lang syne?"

"For days gone by, Rachel," Malcolm whispered, tilting her chin up with his fingers and thumb.

"And for days yet t' come, Malcolm," she answered, her heart in her eyes.

Her three ships had come in: Peace, love, and forgiveness sailed into their lives that night, and Rachel knew all would be well with their souls. Sheltered from the cold in the warmth of Malcolm's arms, she felt her dreams were realized at long last.

Malcolm's lips touched Rachel's tenderly, then more firmly as their kiss deepened into one of shared love and promise.

"For auld lang syne, my jo,
For auld lang syne:
We'll tak' a cup o' kindness yet,
For auld lang syne."

(*jo*: "dear"; *auld lang syne*: "old long since" or "days long ago"— original lyrics by Robert Burns from Scots Musical Museum— 1796, public domain)

STICKY-TOFFEE SCOTTISH PUDDING

PUDDING:

   8 ounces self-rising flour
   1 teaspoon baking powder
   10 ounces boiling water
   6 ounces dates, chopped
   1 teaspoon baking soda
   1 teaspoon vanilla
   2 ounces butter, softened
   6 ounces sugar
   1 egg

Preheat oven to 350°. Sift flour and baking powder in bowl; set aside. To saucepan of boiling water, add dates, baking soda, and vanilla; set aside. Cream butter and sugar in separate bowl; beat in egg and sifted flour mixture. Blend in date mixture. Pour into buttered 9 x 9-inch square baking pan. Bake until firm, about 40 minutes. As pudding cooks, prepare sauce.

SAUCE:

   4 ½ ounces butter
   7 ½ ounces brown sugar
   5 ounces whipping cream

Place ingredients into a saucepan and melt slowly. Boil for one minute. Once pudding is removed from oven, poke a few holes in it with fork, and pour a bit of sauce over top. Place under broiler until it bubbles, but be careful not to let it burn. Serve pudding warm with remaining sauce.

Nollaig chridheil! (Merry Christmas!)

PAMELA GRIFFIN

Pamela Griffin lives in Texas with her family and loves Christmas and all things Gaelic and Celtic. She has a special place in her heart for Scotland and Ireland and hopes to visit those countries one day. She fully gave her life to the Lord after a rebellious young adulthood, and owes the fact that she's alive to a mother who prayed and wouldn't give up faith that God could bring her daughter home to the fold. Because of Pamela's experience, she loves writing stories that inspire, especially about people with flaws, to show how God can work in any life, and that He considers no one hopeless. You're welcome to visit her at: http://www.pamela-griffin.com

A Right, Proper Christmas

by Jill Stengl

Chapter 1

Midlands of England, 1860s

Icy wind cut through Dan's threadbare jacket and drove straight to his bones. Hunching his shoulders and tucking his hands into his armpits, he forged ahead. His feet felt like stinging lumps within his boots. Each breath formed a frosty cloud that settled on his turned-up collar and sculpted icicles on his cap's brim.

He must find shelter for the night. *God, have You noticed Your servant freezing to death?* God had always provided for his needs in the past. . . .

If it's time for me to die, I'm ready. But something

inside him stubbornly clung to life, to the belief that God would provide one more miracle. Why would God call a man to preach, then allow him to die of exposure? That would make no sense.

A sign loomed ahead at the side of the road with LITTLE BRIGHAM—ONE MILE painted on a rough board in white letters. There he might find shelter of some sort, though he had no money and no prospect of earning any. Teeth chattering, he moved on.

Only one year ago, he had looked forward with longing to a Christmas back home in England. But during his absence, his mother had left the old house. And when he did finally locate her living with a butcher on the south side of Birmingham, she had greeted him with an invitation to leave her be and go make a life for himself.

Home? Ha! For him, no such thing existed.

Why, God? Why do I have no love but Yours in my life since Granny died?

Even now, the memory of his mother's hard voice and bitter face made him grimace. Why had he imagined that she would have changed for the better? Why had he thought she might offer him a glimpse of maternal affection just because he returned alive from the Crimean peninsula?

Because he was a fool and dreamer.

God, if any goodness remains on this wicked old earth, please show me, and that soon. I'm nigh on ready to dive into the pit.

He hiked to the top of a rise and looked down upon the village set in a gentle vale. The rectangular tower of a church stood black against the twinkling lights of cottages, rising high enough to block out the lowest stars. Wind whistled past Dan's ears and pushed him forward.

"The church?" he asked aloud. A recent encounter with a sneering bishop back in the city caused him to hesitate. That clergyman had not even tried to conceal his amusement at the suggestion of Dan's ever becoming a minister of the Gospel.

But if the church would not aid the lost and lonely, who would?

He scrunched up his face and shook his head. Stubbornness would be the death of him. "All right then." At the very least, the church building should offer protection from this wind.

As he walked up the church path, a faint cry drifted amid the gravestones. Dan stopped short. A shudder, not caused by cold, rippled through his frame, and the hair on his nape stood on end. Slowly, he let his gaze shift right and turned his head to follow. No ghostly form appeared. He swallowed hard.

Again the thin wail gripped his attention and tightened his throat. This time he pinpointed it to a particular headstone. He took one more step toward the church door, then turned back. Curiosity compelled him to approach that marble slab. Something living must have made that noise.

Teeth clenched, he stepped off the walkway and crunched across frozen sod. A dark form huddled at the base of the gravestone. He touched it with his boot and felt it give. Again he heard the cry. Dan squatted, reached out his hand, and touched cold fur. Gently he moved the creature into full starlight. A cat, its eyes half closed, its teeth bared in a death grimace. The small body was already stiffening.

But as he set it down, something moved and wailed. He felt at the base of the stone again and found a tiny body. A kitten. Two—no, three kittens crouched behind their mother's lifeless form. He picked one up. Its eyes glinted in the starlight, and its mouth opened in a surprisingly loud *meow*.

Without another thought, he tucked two of the kittens into his jacket pockets and the third inside his waistcoat. Rising with a crackle of joints, he continued along the walkway and entered the porch. The door creaked as it opened, then closed behind Dan with a ringing *crash*.

The nave of the church was cold and still. "Hello?" he called. His voice rang hollow in a vast empty space. The clerestory must be very high. Dan reached out in the darkness, moving slowly forward until his hands touched smooth stone. More exploration revealed intricate carvings and the outlines of a human face. He jerked his hand away and shivered. A tomb. He was not yet lonely enough to relish the thought of cozying up to the stone effigy of some departed lord or lady.

Quickly he turned away. As his eyes adjusted, the gray outline of windows appeared high above, and he located rows of pews. Taking care not to squash the kittens, he lay down on a wooden bench and stretched out. If he died during the night, perhaps the townspeople would let his body rest with the remains of their ancestors in the yard. That way at least he would have company on Judgment Day.

An unmarked grave. God would know where his body lay, but no one else. No wife, no family would mourn him. Loneliness gnawed like a canker at his heart.

Only Granny had ever loved him. Almost, he could

feel her gnarled hand on his head and hear her fervent, trembling prayers while he knelt beside her stool in the chimney corner. A love light for him had always shone in Granny's faded eyes, and her faith had been his solid rock.

The kitten inside his waistcoat had curled into a ball against his belly. He felt the tiny vibration of a *purr*. The kitten in his left pocket twisted and turned against his hand and sucked weakly on his fingertip. The kitten in his right pocket didn't move. He cupped its body in his palm and rubbed the soft fur with his fingers.

Heaving a deep sigh, he stared up into darkness. Three motherless babies. He should have left them to freeze. He had nothing to give them but warmth and sympathy.

♪ ♪ ♪

The thatching on Winchell Cottage glimmered in the starlight, rimed with ice. Light glowed in one window. Dame Winchell and her half-wit son would surely enjoy hearing Christmas carols, Charlotte assured herself, although they were unlikely to offer wassail in return.

The boisterous group of carolers assembled in ragged rows. By this time, the youngest among them had lost interest in singing and entertained themselves by punching, poking, and otherwise tormenting each other.

Charlotte's patience ebbed.

"Let us begin with 'Joy to the World,'" she announced in her firmest tone, separating the two Popkin boys, who had engaged in a hair-pulling battle. Why wouldn't the other young adults help her control these children? Charlotte sent Clive Brigham a pleading look, but he was too busy grinning at Hattie Holloway to notice.

Although Charlotte started the song in a comfortable key, two of the singers picked their own range and hurried ahead of the rest. Choosing to ignore them, she closed her eyes and sang her loudest.

The cottage door cracked open. "Ger out," snarled a woman's low voice. "Let a body rest, whyn't ya?"

Several of the older carolers laughed. Little Sally Whitesmith began to cry.

Charlotte drew the child close in a comforting embrace. "We crave pardon for disturbing you, Dame Winchell. We thought only to spread some Christmas ch—"

The door clanked shut. Crestfallen, Charlotte herded her flock away, shushing questions.

"Ain't we done yet, Charlotte?" Sammy Johnston whined. "The wind is awful cold."

"The last house on our list is the rectory," she said.

"The rector mixed up his best wassail for us tonight, and I baked scones, and we'll play blindman's buff."

"Can't we play games first? I'm tired of singing."

The other children echoed Sammy's plea and added, "It's so cold!"

"But don't you see? We must earn our fun by singing the best carols we've sung this night," she said brightly.

Clive and Hattie laughed at some private joke of their own. Charlotte could not even console herself with the possibility that Clive was attempting to make her jealous. Only pride kept her from bursting into frustrated tears. She might as well be invisible for all the notice he took of her.

The day had begun so beautifully. That morning Mother had allowed Charlotte and her three younger sisters to deck the rectory halls with greenery, bows, and candles. Furthermore, she had allowed the girls to bake scones and biscuits, though Christmas Day was yet a week off. Father provided songbooks for the caroling, and he mixed a great pot of steaming wassail. Eighteen youths, girls, and children had assembled for the caroling—including Clive Brigham.

Charlotte had been in love with Clive for almost as long as she could remember. Now, while he was home from Oxford for the holidays, would be an ideal time for him to notice her and realize that she was the woman of his dreams.

That afternoon, when he'd first arrived at the church, the carolers' meeting place, Clive had told Charlotte she looked like a Christmas angel. Her joy had spiraled to giddy heights, even though he did pat her cheek and call her "little sister." It was surely just a term of endearment. They were no blood relation, after all.

But Hattie Holloway had joined the group, looking stylish and lovely in a new bonnet, and ever since then, Clive couldn't seem to take his eyes off her.

George Wendell, one of the bigger boys, grabbed Charlotte by the elbow. "Les and me are going on, Char. We got places to go. It was delightful. Thank you for asking us." He gave Charlotte a broad wink, clucked twice as if she were a horse, and then the two youths jogged up the street before she could draw breath enough to protest.

The icy wind seemed to wrap around her heart. Would Clive desert her, too? He was the last baritone in the group. *Please, God, don't let him leave!*

As Charlotte arranged her remaining singers before the rectory steps, she could scarcely breathe around the lump in her chest. The sight of Hattie's arm linked through Clive's elbow nearly provoked her to tears.

How could he? How could he be so sweet and kind to Charlotte yet flirt openly with Hattie?

"Let us begin with 'Hark! The Herald Angels Sing,'" she said stiffly. Little Sammy surprised her by starting out with a pure, clear "Hark!" and the remaining carolers joined in.

Mother opened the rectory door and called Father to come listen. They stood framed in the light and warmth pouring from the house. A tear trickled down Charlotte's cheek while she sang, "Glory to the newborn King!"

♪ ♪ ♪

Dan felt as if he had no sooner dozed off than a hand gripped his shoulder and shook, hard. "What d'ye mean by sleeping 'ere, man? This be the Lord's 'ouse, not an inn."

"No room at an inn for the likes of me," Dan mumbled, sitting up and blinking in the light of a lantern. "I reckon the good Lord must know how that feels."

The man's broad, black-bearded face split into a grin. "That He do, lad; that He do. Like the foxes, ye've no place to lay yer 'ead. Be that the tale?"

Dan nodded. The kittens were warm and motionless against his fingers.

"Ye've no call to freeze in the church whilst there

be fire and food at the rectory. I 'appen to know the rector will be glad an' all to take ye in. The reverend Mr. Colburn is a kindly man, as like unto the Good Shepherd as earthly man can be. Come wit' me, lad. Ol' Joe'll see ye're fed and bedded down for the night. I've no wish to be diggin' ye a permanent bed in the yard come morning."

Joe wrapped his arm around Dan's shoulders and turned him toward the door. "Just a step once we get outside. O'er the stile and through the 'edgerows. You'll think ye've entered the pearly gates once Miz Colburn takes ye in, lad. A fine woman be that one. And four pretty daughters to charm your eyes whilst ye regains your strength. Been in the army, lad? I thought as much. Ye've the look—worn of heart and bone, and your face that leathered by the sun."

A mist rose among the tombstones and dulled Dan's vision. He saw light ahead, brilliant light that made him blink. Music rang in the darkness—angelic voices proclaiming Christ's birth. Dan stopped in his tracks. "Angels!" he whispered.

"Wha's that you say?" Joe inquired. "Angels? Well, true enough as may be." A deep chuckle rumbled through his chest. "Move along now, lad, and introduce yourself. No call to be shy; you'll be right welcome."

Dan clambered over the stile and staggered toward the light. Shapes appeared through the mist. People bundled against the cold, mostly rosy-faced children, singing bravely in puffs of steam. Carolers! How long had it been since he last heard Christmas carolers? He turned to thank Joe, but the stranger had disappeared without a word of farewell. Or if he had spoken, Dan was too tired and confused to remember.

> *"Now to the Lord sing praises all you within this place,*
> *And with true love and brotherhood each other now*
>   *embrace;*
> *This holy tide of Christmas all others doth efface.*
> *O tidings of comfort and joy, comfort and joy; O tid-*
>   *ings of comfort and joy."*

Her sister Eleanor plucked at Charlotte's elbow and pointed. "I see someone coming. Should I call Father back?"

Charlotte saw the dark figure emerging from the mist of the churchyard. Apprehension tightened her body. "Yes." Eleanor pushed her way inside, making hurried excuses. Mother was welcoming the carolers into the rectory, thanking and greeting the children as they filed past. Charlotte kept a close eye on the approaching man—his halting gait indicated drunken-ness—while she herded her carolers toward the door. Clive had already ushered Hattie inside.

"Mother, please send Father out here." Charlotte tried to keep her voice calm as she followed close behind the last child.

Mother didn't understand her urgency. "He's in the kitchen, child." She trotted after the children, waving her arms and cheerfully calling orders about where to hang up coats and scarves. Chunks of icy mud melted on the entry tiles.

Charlotte nearly pushed Sammy through the door, intending to close it before the stranger could force his way inside. She turned, grasping the door's handle, ready to pull it shut. A man stood on the doorstep, one hand in a frayed fingerless glove clutching a cap to his chest. Charlotte glimpsed his eyes—and could not close the door.

"Is the rector in?" His voice was gruff and raspy.

What to do? She could not ask the man into the parlor where the party was being held. Neither could she leave him out in the cold. "Please step inside. The rector will see you shortly." She held the door open.

"Thank you kindly, miss." He stepped past, and she smelled his unwashed body, but no alcohol. He stopped

129

beside the coat stand already piled with hats, coats, mufflers, and dripping mittens. She saw his wondering gaze flit about the entryway over polished walnut paneling, wreaths and bows on the staircase's banisters, and mirrored candle sconces. "I'd as leave not muss the floor with my dirty boots."

Charlotte allowed herself to smile. "The children have already tracked mud from one end of the house to the other. Would you—would you care for a cup of wassail, sir?"

Gratitude flickered across his smudged features. He had large dark eyes underlined by heavy dark circles as if he not slept in days or weeks. The deep lines cut into his black-whiskered cheeks framed a grim mouth. Yet for all that, it was not an unappealing face.

"You're very kind, miss. I have—kittens." He blinked as if confused.

Charlotte thought she must have misunderstood. "Come again?"

He pulled his hand from his pocket and held out a furry bundle. "Found them in the churchyard. The mother is dead. I. . ." He swayed on his feet, and a dazed expression came over his face.

Charlotte reached out to take the squeaking kitten just as the man's eyes rolled up in his head and he swayed like a falling tree. She rushed forward to catch him, but he was a dead weight in her arms, and she crumpled to the floor. He sprawled across her lap, his head lolling against her shoulder. The kitten scaled her arm like a tree and tried to hide in her hair, its claws raking her neck and ear.

"Father!" she called in a panic. Another kitten poked out its head from beneath the man's waistcoat, stared up at Charlotte, and hissed.

Unhurried footsteps approached the hall. Father paused in the drawing room doorway. Candlelight glinted off his spectacles. "Oh, my dear!" He hastened forward. "Is he alive?"

Chapter 2

T he poor chap looks half starved," a man's quiet voice said. "Let me try the sal volatile."

With a gasp and a start, Dan opened his eyes. The smelling salts' fumes burned his sinuses. He coughed, and pain knifed through his chest.

"He is ill, Father. Whatever will Mother say? But I couldn't leave him outside on a night like this; I simply couldn't!"

So she wasn't a dream after all. He focused on her face.

"I think he is not so much ill as weak from exposure and near starvation—as were his kittens. You did the right thing, Charlotte, my dear." The speaker was a balding man with spectacles perched near the end of his long nose. He wore a clergyman's collar. "What is your name, my friend?"

"Dan Jackson." His voice was a croak.

Dan looked at the girl again. Charlotte. Pink and white skin, soft brown hair in bunches of ringlets near her cheeks, and sparkling eyes tilted up at the corners, giving her a lively air. Angry red scratches marred her white neck.

Remembering, Dan felt the front of his waistcoat.

"Your kittens are safe, Mr. Jackson," Charlotte said. And she smiled. Dan looked away, feeling dizzy all over again.

"I am Mr. Colburn, rector here in Little Brigham." While speaking, the rector rose from his knees and settled into a side chair. "And this is my eldest daughter, Charlotte."

Dan glanced around. He lay on a settee in a small study, bundled beneath a thick woolen blanket. A small fire glowed on the hearth, and an oil lamp glowed on the desk. Charlotte sat near his feet; the rector sat near his head.

"I swooned?"

"You most certainly did. Where do you come from, Mr. Jackson?"

"From Birmingham, most recent." His head felt thick.

"Never done that afore—swoon, I mean."

"The Crimea before that?"

"Yes, sir."

"I thought as much. You seem stretched thin of spirit and soul. Were you wounded?"

"Only a few scratches, since healed."

His gaze returned to Charlotte's neck, and she smiled again, this time with amusement. "Scratches can be painful," she said.

"When did you last eat?" the rector inquired softly.

Dan shifted his gaze to the fire. "I don't recall. Two days, maybe. Times are bad in the city. I headed south on a canal barge, but ran out of money. Offered to work my way. No luck. So I walked."

"Until tonight," Charlotte said in a near whisper.

"Until tonight. I found a dead cat in the churchyard and picked up its kittens. A fool act. I had naught to offer."

"Except kindness and warmth," Charlotte said. "It was a Christmas thing to do."

"Charlotte dear, will you fetch our guest some food and drink?" the rector suggested.

"Yes, Father." She rose, paused to look down at Dan, then walked from the room, her full skirts rustling.

Dan forced his gaze back to the rector's face. "A

party of people—I saw them come inside. Singers."

The rector smiled. "Yes, my daughters prepared a party for the carolers."

"I should go. You have guests. She should be with them." Dan made a move to rise, but the rector gently stopped him.

"Your presence gives us only pleasure, Mr. Jackson. If my daughter did not wish to bring you food, she would have said as much. She is a forthright young woman, yet she has a kind heart," Mr. Colburn remarked. "Are you married, Mr. Jackson?"

Dan felt his face grow warm. The rector had seen him looking at Charlotte.

"No, sir. Few decent women in the Crimea, and the good Lord kept me from the other kind. You needn't fear; your daughter is beyond my touch, and I wouldn't presume to think elsewise." He coughed, then continued, "I hope sometime to marry and have family, but first a man's got to find work. You wouldn't know of an opening hereabouts, would you now?"

The rector pursed his lips and wrinkled his forehead. "Times are hard everywhere, Mr. Jackson. But I shall keep my ears open. Do you have experience?"

"I was an 'ostler before I went to war, and I worked for the cavalry in the Crimea. Horses are my only skill, though I haven't got so much as a swayback nag to my name." He tried to smile. "Just cats."

"Horses." The rector rubbed his chin and pondered. "A useful skill. We shall see."

Charlotte hurried back into the room. "I set soup on to boil for you, Mr. Jackson, but I thought a scone or two might hold you until the soup is ready." She offered a plate of raisin scones with thick cream. "And Father's wassail."

He took the steaming cup and the plate from her hands. "Thank you kindly, miss." He met her gaze.

She sat down abruptly. "I fed the kittens in the kitchen and put them in a basket near the stove. They're sleeping."

"Good." He felt self-conscious about eating while she watched, but hunger overcame his qualms. The scones filled the edges of his aching void, and the spicy wassail warmed him from the inside out.

"How did you find us?" Charlotte asked.

He gulped the last drop and wiped his hand across his mouth. Too late he remembered his napkin. "I saw the church and thought I might sleep inside for the night." He shook his head to drive off a creeping lethargy. "But your sexton found me sleeping on the pew and told me to come here. He showed me the way through the churchyard and over the stile."

The rector and his daughter exchanged glances.

"I heard singing and thought it was angels." Dan heard his voice begin to slur. "God sent me to the light. Found an angel."

♪ ♪ ♪

Charlotte watched Dan's head sag to one side. His deep breathing filled the silence. "I fear he won't want his soup tonight," she said.

Her father smiled. "I believe you're right. I hope he doesn't wake cramped after sleeping on that settee. It's barely long enough for him, though he isn't a tall man. I wonder who directed him here. Odd—we have no sexton at present."

"Do you think he'll be warm enough?" Charlotte rose with her father but lingered, studying that shadowed face. "The poor man."

"I shall stoke the fire before I retire for the night." Father patted her shoulder. "You should attend your remaining guests, my dear."

She gasped. "Oh, the carolers! I completely forgot them." Picking up her skirts, she hurried away. What might Clive and Hattie have done in her absence? How could she have allowed a common stranger to distract her from things of genuine importance? Things such as winning back the interest of her future husband.

♪ ♪ ♪

Charlotte, her three sisters, and their mother sat around the parlor, staring blankly at the party clutter their guests had left behind. "Clive kissed Hattie under the kissing ball," Priscilla announced.

Charlotte's heart gave a painful wrench.

"Only on the cheek, silly," Priscilla's twin, Drusilla, corrected with a knowing air.

"It was still a kiss, and Charlotte's jealous."

"Young ladies, we do not speak of such things," Mother said firmly. "Help your sisters carry out the dishes."

"Why can't Molly do that in the morning?" Drusilla grumbled.

"Molly does enough work around this house to earn twice what we can afford to pay her. I have four daughters with strong, healthy bodies, and there is no good reason on this earth why they cannot do honest labor." Mother set the example by carrying out a tray loaded with empty cups and tumblers.

Charlotte began stacking plates. "I used to grumble about Mother making us learn how to run a household by doing all the work ourselves, so I know just how you feel, Dru. But now that I am older—"

"Do, please, spare us the now-that-I-am-older-and-wiser speech, Charlotte," Eleanor said. "If you marry Clive Brigham, you'll never need to lift a finger. No blacking stoves, no polishing fire irons for you. You'll have an army of servants at your beck and call."

"But Clive didn't kiss Char, he kissed Hattie," Priscilla said, "even though she does have freckles."

"I have a surprise for you in the kitchen," Charlotte said. "Something cute and furry."

The twins instantly fell for the diversion and pelted her with excited questions.

After the clutter had been cleared away and the kittens were bedded down for the night, Charlotte climbed the stairs, watching her hand slide up the polished walnut banister. Heaviness seemed to weigh down her spirit. Where had the joy gone? No matter how hard she tried to recapture the spirit of Christmas, nothing brought back the joy she remembered so vividly from her childhood holidays.

Inside her tiny bedchamber, she set her lamp on her dressing table, sat down, and regarded her reflection. Earlier in the day she had gazed into her mirrored eyes with confidence and anticipation, knowing that she looked attractive. Real-lace flounces and tiny tucks on the bodice of her burgundy gown enhanced her curves, and a wide sash hugged her waist. Fashion and cold weather dictated the necessity of multiple flannel petticoats which added inches to her waistline, but then, Hattie's waist was no slimmer.

She pulled pins from her hair and shook her head. Glossy locks tumbled down her back.

Clive, why do you ignore me? He was so handsome and aristocratic with his flashing smile, his gray-blue eyes, and his smooth, yellow hair. He could not be in love with Hattie—could he? What was Hattie's secret? Charlotte considered asking her mother how a woman contrived to fascinate a man, but Mother would only read her a lecture about modesty and propriety, and adjure her to trust in the Lord.

Christmas this year simply must be perfect. Tonight the children had been uncooperative, and then the stranger's arrival had distracted Charlotte from her purpose. But she would have other opportunities to impress Clive before he returned to college. She loved that boy with a passion that nearly consumed her—surely he must respond sooner or later! Somehow she must show him a glimpse of the cozy, comfortable home they two could share if only he would marry her. . . .

Kneeling on the bed, she pulled its curtains closed. Her sheets felt clammy as she gingerly slid her toes, her feet, and her legs down beneath her covers. Would the stranger sleeping downstairs be warm enough?

Cold feet drove away sleep. She tucked up her legs and curled into a ball.

A dog barked somewhere in the distance. *Mother should let us get a dog to guard against intruders.*

Like Dan Jackson.

And kittens.

She chuckled softly, picturing that little furry head bobbing from beneath the man's waistcoat. The waistcoat also concealed a tender heart. Yet, such a coarse manner of speaking he had. Poorly educated.

What if he wakes in the night and walks out with Mother's silver candlesticks?

Such a nice, deep voice. A kind voice.

Could be a murderer.

Such beautiful dark eyes. . .

♪ ♪ ♪

Clang. Clatter.

Dan sat up, blinking.

A figure rose from the fireside. "I beg your pardon, Mr. Jackson. I intended to sneak in here and stoke your fire before our maid arrives this morning, but I am as stealthy as cannon fire, apparently." The reverend Mr. Colburn smiled in apology.

"This is your study. I'll be on my way."

"Nonsense, lad. You should remain where you are. Your voice sounds congested. Are you feverish?"

Dan pondered his condition for a moment. "I feel weak." His voice caught; he coughed a sharp, barking cough and winced at the pain of it.

"Ah, Mrs. Colburn will make a poultice that should draw out that cough. She'll be here in a trice, if I'm not greatly mistaken."

Shoes clicked in the hallway, and a woman's harried yet pleasant face peeked around the door. "May I enter?"

"You may enter, my dear," Mr. Colburn said. "Did you hear his cough?"

"I did, Mr. Colburn, and I know just the treatment." She bustled forward and placed her hand on Dan's forehead. "I am Mrs. Colburn, of course. You are most welcome in our home, and I trust you will stay as long as your needs require."

Dan recognized sincerity in the woman's soft brown eyes. Charlotte had not inherited her beauty from her mother, yet Dan saw family resemblance. "Thank you, ma'am." He could manage no more without coughing.

"We must move our guest to a bedchamber where he will not be disturbed," she declared. "I'll have Charlotte move in with Eleanor."

Guest! Dan wanted to protest, but his voice would not cooperate. Shivering, he lay back on the settee and huddled beneath the blanket. The notion of staying on as a guest in this warm and welcoming household struck him as nearly ideal.

♪ ♪ ♪

Mr. Jackson asked to take a bath before he set foot upstairs. Mother feared he would take a chill and die, but he insisted, so she enlisted Charlotte, Molly the housemaid, and the twins to haul water from the cistern into the scullery. Eleanor escaped the chore by pleading a headache.

"This bucket is too heavy for me," Priscilla grumbled. She switched its weight from one hand to the other. Water splashed over her feet.

"Mr. Jackson will appreciate your help," Charlotte assured her.

"Why should I care? Eleanor says he's just a beggar."

Charlotte stopped to glare at her little sister. "That is unkind. He is our guest, and we shall treat him like visiting royalty. As Father often says, 'We may be hosting an angel, unaware.' Do your work to please Jesus."

Despite their parents' careful training and frequent admonitions, Priscilla followed Eleanor's lead and seemed to delight in making everyone else's life difficult. Drusilla, the quieter twin, emulated Charlotte.

Priscilla snorted. "Little wonder Clive prefers Hattie to you. She doesn't preach sermons at him three times a day." She grimaced and stuck out her tongue.

Heat rushed to Charlotte's face. She set down her buckets, grabbed the girl's arm, and drew a deep breath for a scathing retort. Her hand itched with desire to slap the smug look off Priscilla's face.

Slow footsteps approached from the hall. Mr. Jackson appeared in the doorway, his expression hesitant.

The two sisters stared at him in shamed silence. Drusilla emerged from the scullery with an empty pail and asked, "What's wrong?" Molly appeared in the doorway behind her, looking equally curious.

Charlotte released Priscilla and felt her face burn hotter than ever. "Not a thing. Please sit here while we finish, Mr. Jackson. It will be only a few minutes more." She copied her mother's most gracious manner.

He sat carefully on one of the kitchen stools.

"Do you want to see the kitties?" Drusilla asked,

looking directly up into his face. "One of them is kind of weak and doesn't move much, but the other two are lively. We call them Fluffy, Fuzzy, and Purr because we don't know if they're boys or girls."

He smiled and nodded slightly. Drusilla ran to the stove and pulled the basket from behind it. Making a pouch of her apron, she bundled the kittens into it and returned to him.

Mr. Jackson lifted one kitten, checked under its tail, and set it on his knee. He inspected each protesting kitten in turn, then stroked all three furry backs with one sweep of his hand. "Three brothers," he said hoarsely and turned his head to cough.

The harsh sound of that cough made Charlotte frown.

"They eat lamb if we grind it up good and add broth. Charlotte told us to try goats' milk, and they suck it up pretty well. They want to suck everything, though," Drusilla told him.

Priscilla appeared at his other side and took one of the kittens. "This one is my favorite. Father found the dead mother cat and buried it behind our stable. He said she was black with white paws, like this kitten."

Drusilla held up another kitten. "This one is dressed like a bishop. He's the quiet one. I want to call him

Harvey now that I know he's a boy."

A smile softened Mr. Jackson's face. He lifted the third kitten. "Mine looks like a butler with a high white collar. Humphrey."

Priscilla grinned. "Mine is Hubert."

"On'y the hot water is yet needed, miss," Molly said, as she again returned from the scullery carrying an empty bucket. "D'you want that I should fetch it?"

Charlotte felt blood rush into her face; she had neglected her work to watch the little scene. "I'll get it, Molly. You go ahead with your regular chores. Thank you."

Molly gave her a genuine smile. "You ain't never no trouble, miss."

Charlotte used two towels to protect her hands and lifted a steaming kettle from the stovetop. Mr. Jackson returned his kitten to Drusilla and started to rise, his expression troubled.

"Don't worry; I can do this. I'm stronger than I look," Charlotte assured him. "You just rest there." After emptying two kettles into the tub, she tested the temperature. Good and hot.

"Your bath is ready, Mr. Jackson!" she called. "The soap and towels are close at hand, and Father left a razor for your use." She met his gaze as she stepped into the kitchen, drying her hands on her apron.

"Thank you, miss. Me being so dirty—I couldn't—" He coughed again. "Your room, I—" Another bout of coughing bent him over.

Priscilla and Drusilla stared at him, frightened, the kittens clutched in their arms.

At last he looked up, shivering, eyes watering, and Charlotte felt tears burn her own eyes. "You poor man, I think you should just go straight to bed. Sheets and blankets will wash."

He shook his head, closed his eyes, and pinched the bridge of his nose. "I'll rest better once I'm clean. Like Mr. Wesley said, 'Cleanliness is next to godliness.' "

While Mr. Jackson bathed downstairs, Mrs. Colburn and her two oldest daughters quickly turned Charlotte's bedchamber into a sickroom. They aired clean sheets before the peat fire glowing on the hearth in order to remove any lingering dampness, turned and plumped the feather bolster, then made the bed. Eleanor had already brought up a pitcher of well water and a clean tumbler to set on the bedside table. When the entire chamber smelled fresh and every last speck of dust or dirt had been eradicated, Mrs. Colburn pronounced it good and headed downstairs.

Charlotte glanced around her room, looking for

anything else she might want or need during her stay in Eleanor's room. Would the guest be comfortable here? Would he enjoy sleeping in her bedchamber with its ruffles and lace and the strong scent of lavender?

A silly thought. Why should he care? Dan Jackson might be married and have several children, for all she knew. He looked to be a hard sort of man, the type that would scorn frills and furbelows. Then she pictured him with that kitten cradled in his big hands, and a smile touched her lips once more.

Judging by the clamor and activity below, Mr. Jackson was now on his way upstairs. Charlotte smoothed the pillows and the counterpane, then hurried to the head of the staircase. Mr. Jackson had one arm over Father's shoulder, and he wore one of Father's nightshirts and an old bed gown. Daylight from the staircase window caught in his damp, tousled hair and reflected off Father's bald head as they climbed one slow step at a time.

Mr. Jackson glanced up as they passed her on the landing, but no recognition glimmered in his eyes. He appeared drawn and exhausted. The shadows beneath his eyes looked stark on his clean-shaven face, no longer blended with soot and grime.

"Charlotte!" Mother's exclamation spun Charlotte

around. "Child, have you no delicacy? Get to your room and stay there."

Charlotte wanted to protest—she was nineteen years old, no longer a child—but she hastened off to Eleanor's bedchamber.

Chapter 3

Dan awakened, feeling motion on the bed. His eyes opened, but he saw no one. Another little *thump*. He turned his head to one side and looked into a kitten's startled face. It froze.

He smiled and tried to speak. "Hello." To a kitten, that raspy voice probably sounded like a monster's snarl. His arms were tangled in the bed sheets. He found a way to get one hand free and reached for the kitten. It was too young to run far; it squalled as he lifted it.

He settled the little creature on his chest and began to rub its head and neck with his thumb. Almost immediately it began to purr.

From beyond the bed curtains he heard a whisper: "What are you doing in here? If Mother finds out, you'll not sit down for a week!"

"No, no—he likes it!"

"He likes what? Priscilla, did you wake Mr. Jackson?"

Dan saw the curtains rustle. The child must have been watching him through a gap.

"I didn't wake him, Char. Humphrey did."

"Humphrey? You brought one of the kittens in here? Oh, Pris, what will Mother say?"

"But he likes it, don't you, Mr. Jackson?"

"I do," Dan croaked. He weakly pulled the curtain aside, hoping for a glimpse of Charlotte.

Priscilla smirked at him, her eyes alight. "I thought you would want to see Humphrey. He eats almost as much as Hubert does. Harvey is the smallest. They're all three quite intelligent. Father brought in a tray full of sandy dirt, and they know just how to use it."

Dan smiled. His eyes hurt, but he felt significantly better. "How long have I been sleeping?" He had lost track of time since the rector helped him into this bed. For all he knew, Christmas had come and gone, and the New Year, as well. He had slept away the hours, waking only for meals and necessities.

To his satisfaction, Charlotte pulled the curtain farther back along its rail. "You came to us two days ago. This is Sunday. Mother says you were out of your head for a time yesterday, talking to invisible people. But other times you were lucid."

"I don't remember." A feeling of warm pleasure crept through him. He wished for more light, the better to see her shining hair and smooth cheeks.

The kitten curled up beneath Dan's chin, still purring. Its tiny paws kneaded his neck, its claws like tiny pinpricks. He saw Charlotte's lips curve into a sweet smile as she watched.

"Do you want me to bring Harvey and Hubert, too?" Priscilla asked.

"Maybe later." Dan was already getting sleepy. "Do I have a fever?"

Charlotte laid her hand along his cheek. He closed his eyes. "You feel warm, but you're no longer burning up. Father nearly called in the physician, but Mother told him to let you sleep. She said your own strength would best fight this fever."

"I'm hungry."

"Good! I'll try to bring you some food. You stay here, Priscilla. I'll tell Mother you're awake, Mr. Jackson." Charlotte rubbed her hands down her apron, smiled again, and hurried from the room.

"Would you open the bed curtains?" he asked Priscilla.

The girl leaped into action. Soon, winter daylight spilled across the bed. Dan looked around the room, really seeing it for the first time—a small, gabled chamber with whitewashed walls and a warped wooden floor. Heavy, old-fashioned walnut furniture should have given the room a sober aspect, but white ruffles and embroidered flowers softened the effect. Pink, purple, blue, yellow—bright blooms of every hue were sprinkled across the counterpane, the bed curtains, and the pillow tops. Someone had even painted flowers on the wall like a little garden.

The door opened, and Mrs. Colburn entered. "I beg your pardon for the intrusion, Mr. Jackson. Priscilla is a lively child, and Charlotte cannot seem to restrain her. Priscilla, remove that animal from this room!"

Dan covered the kitten with his hand. "Please leave him. He—he keeps me warm."

As if the tiny body offered significant heat.

Mrs. Colburn lifted one brow. "I hope you are not feeling worse." She laid her slightly clammy hand on his forehead.

"No, ma'am. I could get up, I think." He wanted to cough, but restrained it, fearing he would disturb the kitten.

"Really?" She stared into his eyes. "You do look and

sound much better. But I'll have you know, you were a very sick young man, Mr. Jackson. The Lord brought you to us for good reason."

"Yes, ma'am, and I'm grateful to Him and you both."

"I think you should wait until tomorrow before you attempt coming downstairs, but you might sit beside the fire here. Oh, the fire has nearly gone out! Molly!" She called through the door. "Where is that girl?" She left the room and called down the staircase. "Charlotte, tell Molly to bring peat! What? She's gone home? Then you bring it up, or send Eleanor! Mr. Jackson's fire is dying, and it's cold in this room!"

Dan closed his eyes while she bustled about.

"Are you very hungry?"

He looked up. "Yes, ma'am. Dreadful hungry."

"Then I'll fetch your tea."

She vanished into the hallway. Dan dozed until he heard footsteps on the stairs. Charlotte appeared, toting a lumpy sack. She glanced his way and smiled. "I hope Priscilla and I didn't bother you too very much."

"You bothered me not in the slightest." He could speak proper English when he made an effort. The kitten slept on, ignoring the rumbling voice coming from its sleeping spot.

Charlotte knelt beside the hearth and carefully

arranged peat bricks on the grating. "Mother is unhappy about the kitten in your sickroom. She gave Priscilla a talking-to."

"I like having him here."

She smiled at him over her shoulder. "The twins insist that the kittens have no fleas."

"Glad I am to hear it. What will your family do tonight?"

"Probably sit in the kitchen and read. We try not to work on the Sabbath. Father believes our day of rest should be pleasant and restful, not onerous. Most evenings we do handwork while Father reads aloud. I am making knitted mufflers and lace cuffs for Christmas gifts." She poked at the peat and blew on the embers.

"My grandmother tatted lace."

"Did you live with your grandmother?"

"She lived with us until she died five years ago. My mother worked, so Granny mostly raised me. She was a fine Christian woman."

Charlotte settled back to sit on her heels. "My grandparents are all dead now, but I dearly loved my grandmum Colburn. She taught me to make crocheted lace. What did your father do?"

"I never knew my father." He steered the subject back to handwork. "Did you make all these pillows and things?" He waved his hand to indicate the room's decorations.

She looked slightly embarrassed. "I did."

"I thought as much. And you painted the walls?"

She nodded. "It's silly, I know, but I do love flowers."

"I like it. Makes the room feel like springtime. Like you." He captured her gaze and held on until he thought his heart might give out.

At last she looked away, color flooding her cheeks. "I must go, Mr. Jackson. I'll send one of the twins up to take the kitten soon. I hope you recover quickly." She scrambled up and left the room.

Later that evening, the twins sneaked all three kittens upstairs. Dan sat up in bed and watched the tiny brothers tumble, squeak, stalk, and pounce upon each other. Their pink paws and pink noses contrasted with their fuzzy black coats and white markings.

"All three the same colors, yet each so different from his brothers," he commented after Drusilla rescued her Harvey from a mock attack by Humphrey. "Just as you twins are alike yet different."

The two girls had climbed up on the foot of the bed to play with the kittens. Dan thought their mother would undoubtedly object, but the girls ignored his subtle hints. He scooped up his favorite kitten and held it near his face. Solemn gray blue eyes gazed into his, and the kitten patted his nose.

"Humphrey says he's sleepy and needs his supper. Best take all three down to the kitchen afore your mother finds you here," he said. "I thought Sunday evening was a time for quiet reading."

Drusilla frowned at him. "Mother fell asleep, and Father is out visiting a sick parishioner. We're having fun, and Harvey isn't sleepy."

"Neither is Hubert." Priscilla lifted the kitten, and her apron came with it. "Hubert, let go." The kitten mewled and held tighter. One by one she released its claws from her apron. Tiny snags marked the fabric.

"Girls, Mr. Jackson is the tired one." Charlotte suddenly stepped into the room. Had she been watching from the hallway? Without one glance at Dan, she started fussing with the fire. "You need to be thoughtful of his wishes and take the kittens downstairs now."

Priscilla looked quickly at Dan, and she must have seen exhaustion in his face, for her shoulders slumped. "Oh, very well. We'll bring them back tomorrow, Mr. Jackson. Humphrey misses you when he's in the kitchen." She picked up two kittens and slid off the bed. Drusilla clutched her Harvey and followed.

"And I'll miss him. Thanks for the company." He

listened to the clatter of their shoes on the stairs before he said, "And thanks to you for the rescue, miss."

Charlotte faced him, rubbing her hands down her apron. "Do you need water or food or anything else tonight?" She sounded breathless.

He paused to study her, then slowly shook his head. "I meant no harm; they climbed on the bed without my leave and stayed—"

"Mr. Jackson, I know my sisters. You need make no explanation. Thank you for your patience with them, and I'll do my best to prevent a repeat invasion."

Relieved, he rested back against the pillows and spoke in his best English. "They're no real bother, but I'm right sure your parents would disapprove—as they should. Your family is what God must have intended a family to be. I'm thankful to have made your acquaintance. I'd nigh given up on life and love afore I met you."

♪ ♪ ♪

Charlotte quietly closed the sickroom door and leaned her forehead against its panels. Her heart raced, and her chest felt tight. Never, ever should she have sent the twins away as if maneuvering to be alone with Mr. Jackson! As soon as the girls left the room, she had become intensely aware of him, a strange man sitting on her bed in Father's nightshirt, with her knitted green bed scarf draped incongruously over his shoulders. Although he had said and done nothing untoward, the room had suddenly become small and stifling.

This stranger brought out astonishing feelings—reactions no man had ever induced in her before, not even Clive. She felt feminine and alive, yet also somewhat frightened. Not so much of him as of herself.

Slowly she moved along the hall and entered Eleanor's room. The fire had burned low, so she poked it back into life and added fuel. Then, seating herself at the dressing table, she pulled out her hairpins and stared at the floor.

How many men would react so mildly to a pair of intrusive little girls? When Charlotte first glimpsed her sisters through the open chamber door—the two of them and three kittens clambering about on the sick stranger's bed—her heart had nearly stopped. Of all the foolish, ignorant tricks!

Yet she had paused to observe and found herself amazed by his patience. More than once he had hinted that the children should get off the bed and take the kittens downstairs, but never had he raised his voice or spoken unkindly. No suggestion of disrespect entered his voice, words, or gaze.

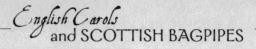

What an unusual man! If only he were more than an unemployed ex-soldier of no social standing. If only—if only Clive had such velvety dark eyes full of mystery and magic.

Chapter 4

The following afternoon, Dan washed at his basin then pulled on an oversized pair of trousers and a faded wool tunic that someone had left folded on a chair in one corner of the room. The tunic hung on his frame, its sleeves were too short, and the fabric abraded his skin. He wrapped the bed scarf around his shoulders, glanced at his reflection in Charlotte's dressing-table mirror, and laughed aloud. Like an incredibly ugly woman he looked in that scarf, with his black growth of whiskers and wildly insubordinate hair.

His limbs were shaky; otherwise he felt good. He could breathe deeply without breaking into a fit of coughing.

Slowly he descended the staircase, mistrustful of his rubbery knees. The house seemed empty, yet he heard voices from somewhere.

He headed toward the back of the house and entered the kitchen. Laundry dried on racks before the fireplace, and the room had a humid, misty atmosphere. He smelled soap and bluing. Following the clatter of a mangle and the hiss of steam, he peered through the doorway of the scullery where he had bathed days earlier.

The small room seemed filled with laboring females. Not one of them noticed Dan. All were clad in cotton shifts and faded old skirts, their sleeves rolled up against the oppressive heat. Charlotte lifted dripping garments from a steaming copper and stacked them near the mangle, which Mrs. Colburn operated, cranking the garments through, one at time, to wring out excess water. Sweat beaded on Charlotte's flushed face, and damp hair stuck to her cheeks and neck.

Feeling like an intruder, Dan backed away unseen and sought out the rector's study. He knocked on the closed door.

"Enter."

Mr. Colburn looked up from his desk and rose to his feet as Dan stepped into the room. "Ah, what joy to see you on your feet, Mr. Jackson!"

"Call me Dan, if you please, sir."

"Does my wife know you are up and about?" The rector's eyes held a conspiratorial glint. He pulled two chairs close to the fire. As soon as Dan sank into one armchair, the rector sat across from him.

"No sir, although she said last night that I might get up today. I found your womenfolk doing laundry. Thought I might best help by standing clear."

Mr. Colburn laughed aloud. "Perspicacious of you, son."

Dan grinned and scratched his forearm where the tunic's sleeve rubbed his skin. "I'm that if you say so, sir."

The rector's smile changed into a considering look. "It means you are perceptive. Things that others might not observe, you see clearly. How much schooling did you receive, Dan Jackson?"

"I did four years at the National School but never took my exams. My Greek and Latin are weak. I know geography and sciences from reading, and I can use proper grammar if I set my mind to it. My officer on the peninsula, Major Sykes, brought half his library with him and gave me leave to use it."

"Indeed." The minister spoke slowly, as if thinking deep thoughts. "Are you well acquainted with the Holy Scriptures?"

"I first learned to read from my grandmother's Bible, sir. I can quote whole psalms and list every book of the Canon in order. I still know my catechism." He coughed. "More than anything, I wish I could study more about God."

"Do you now?" Mr. Colburn looked gratified. "For your own edification only, or for some greater purpose?"

Dan rubbed the back of his neck. "My heart is burdened for my people back home in Birmingham. Most have no way of hearing the gospel. Sure, there are churches in town, but none close enough. People haven't got time nor strength to travel far to hear a preacher. I told them what I know, for sure, and some I've led to Christ's salvation, but I need more training in the deeper things. The people need more than the weak 'milk of the Word' I can give them."

The rector studied him with shining, yet sober, eyes. "Daniel Jackson, I believe you've heard the Macedonian call—although in your case 'tis the Birminghamian call. You're an evangelist by the Lord's almighty power and gifting."

"I hear His call but have no way to answer it. No college would take me, so I've no chance of wearing a collar like yours. My speech is rough, and I've no proper manners." Yet Dan felt a flutter of excitement. If God called, would He not also grant the means to answer?

"You are exactly the right messenger for the people you're called to serve," the rector said firmly. "God is never mistaken about these things. If 'tis only training you lack, I'll gladly share my meager store of knowledge. Your fervor inspires me, son. Why should I not be Paul to your Apollos?"

Dan lifted his brows, uncertain of the analogy. "Why not indeed, sir?"

Mr. Colburn chuckled. "Soon you'll fully understand my meaning. Dan, I offer you full access to my library for as long as you need it. Take books back up to your room if you like, or remain here and discuss them with me. And one thing is certain: We must find you proper clothing before you appear in public. An ascetic monk craving self-abasement would doubtless prize that tunic, but no guest in this home should be subjected to such humiliation."

Dan scratched at his collarbone and silently agreed.

"You may have my spare razor, and I'll find you a more comfortable shirt while you peruse the bookshelves." The rector rose. "If you enjoy reading aloud, you'll find an appreciative audience this evening."

♪ ♩ ♪

Mrs. Colburn and her daughters gathered around the

hearth in the sitting room, pursuing their fancywork by the glow of an oil lamp on the side table. Charlotte's fingers flew as she crocheted the last inch of an intricate cuff intended as Molly the housemaid's Boxing Day gift, but only half her mind focused on her work.

The muffler she had knitted for Clive kept dangling into her thoughts. Clive already owned several mufflers. As eldest son and heir of the local squire, he lacked for no possible creature comforts.

Mr. Jackson would make much better use of a thick woolen muffler. Charlotte might possibly even eke out a pair of mittens from the leftover yarn. If Mr. Jackson departed the rectory before Christmas Day, she could bestow them upon him as parting gifts. Charity gifts, of course.

But then what gift could she offer Clive to make him see her ideal-wife qualities? She could bake treacle-ginger biscuits, her own special recipe. Or pecan pastry with black currant filling. Clive was fond of sweets—perhaps a bit fonder than was good for him. However, to his way of thinking, baking was servants' work. He would probably mock her efforts and accuse of her aspiring to hire out as someone's cook.

According to Father, Mr. Jackson's childhood had been nearly devoid of treats like biscuits and tarts.

Charlotte recalled his obvious enjoyment of her scones that first evening. . . .

"Why are you smiling, Char?" Priscilla asked. "You look smug."

Charlotte's smile vanished. "I simply enjoy my work, that's all." She glanced up and leaped to her feet. Thread and needles dropped from her lap.

Dan Jackson stood in the sitting room doorway, clad in baggy trousers and an old shirt and waistcoat of her father's. He held a book and wore a hopeful expression.

"This is a sewing circle," Eleanor said in unwelcoming tones.

Dan brushed hair out of his eyes. "No men allowed? I'll be off then. Sorry to intrude."

Mother found her voice. "Mr. Jackson, certainly you may join us. But should you be out of bed?"

"I'd go stark mad if I stayed there any longer," he said, coughing a little. "Thank you for washing my clothes. I saw them hung up in the kitchen."

"You are most welcome, Mr. Jackson."

Charlotte seconded her mother's statement with a quick nod and a smile. "On Monday nights the house always feels damp, except by the fire. And our hands are wrinkled and chapped from the water." She held up her own reddened hands, realizing that she would have hidden them from Clive. To Mr. Jackson she somehow wanted to prove her usefulness around a household.

"You carry a book." She indicated the volume in his hand. "Might you read aloud to us?" Or would such a request embarrass him?

But he nodded. "Sure. That's why I brought it: *A Christmas Carol.*"

"Charlotte is mad about that book," Eleanor said. "It's like the Bible to her."

"Eleanor, do not be blasphemous. Drusilla, bring Mr. Jackson a chair," Mother ordered.

"I'll do it, Mother, since I'm already up." Charlotte stepped over Eleanor's feet and brought one of the side chairs into their circle, close to the fire screen.

"Thank you." He moved forward so quickly that their shoulders brushed. He smelled nice, he had shaved, and his hair was combed. It was still too long, and it stuck up in places, but he had made an attempt.

"On Christmas Day we're having a party of friends and family. If you're feeling well enough by then, I trust you will join us, Mr. Jackson," Mother said. "Our dinners are never formal affairs. We simply enjoy the good company and fellowship."

"Thank you kindly, ma'am."

"We intend to host a proper Christmas party this

year," Charlotte added. "With all the traditional foods and games, like Mr. Dickens writes about."

"I like Dickens," he said quietly. "Especially this book." He held up the thin volume. "I used to read his books aloud to my grandmother. Before that, she read them aloud to me."

"Then you understand the importance of preserving our holiday traditions," Charlotte said with a pleased smile.

"Charlotte is fanatical about this; but then Charlotte is fanatical about nearly everything," Eleanor said, sighing. "I am Eleanor; I'm fourteen. I know you're Mr. Jackson."

"Call me Dan." He scanned the twins. "No kittens tonight?"

"They attack our threads and yarns and snag things," Drusilla explained.

"Mayhap we could visit them once you're finished working. Should I read now? I should think we all know the start of it." He opened the book carefully, turned the first few pages, then slid his big hand gently down the page. Before reading the first line he glanced up once more and caught Charlotte's gaze. Again she smiled. She couldn't help it—he was just so nice.

He coughed softly then began. " 'Marley was dead: to begin with. There is no doubt whatever about that.' "

Chapter 5

Christmas dinner at the Colburn house was unlike anything Dan had ever before experienced. Squire Brigham was in attendance along with his wife, a son, and a daughter near Eleanor's age. An elderly spinster and her widowed sister also joined the party, and then there was Dan.

Scarcely a square inch of tablecloth could be seen between the myriad serving trays piled with food. An immense roasted turkey graced the center of the dining table. A rabbit stuffed with oysters held down one end of the table, balanced by a large baked fish at the other. Oranges and grapes spilled from a silver bowl. Tarts, biscuits, sauces, pastries, jellies, and buns filled every available space.

Dan mostly sat quietly and observed. Seated at the rector's left hand, across the table from the squire, and beside old Mrs. Benton who was slightly deaf, he occupied himself by tasting moderate portions of each dish. He overheard snatches of conversation from the far end of the table; Charlotte kept up a lively banter with Master Clive Brigham, seated across from her. Dan could see the young man's grinning face and hear his occasional quip.

Clive was tall, handsome, wealthy, educated, articulate, and seemed to be sincerely fond of Charlotte Colburn. She deserved a man like him. She deserved the best of everything.

That pain in Dan's chest must be lingering effects of his illness. Instead of Christmas peace and good cheer, he felt a heaviness of spirit. All these rich trappings— the greenery, the red velvet ribbons, the candlelight, and the colorful fruit—none of them brought back the quiet joy he had experienced earlier that day at the Christmas church service.

The rector had read the Christmas story from the Gospels of Luke and Matthew, and the worshipers had sung a few carols. Sharing a songbook with Drusilla, Dan had glanced over the child's head and met Charlotte's smiling gaze more than once. Joy welled up in his spirit, as well as thanksgiving, for God's provision, for His Son, and especially for the company of one lovely young woman.

How beautiful she was in a gown of deep green! A crocheted-lace collar accented her delicate features and soft-looking skin. "Eyes like doves"—where had he heard that poetic description? It suited Charlotte. All day long he had struggled to keep his gaze averted; all too often he had failed.

Now Dan fervently wished for the day to end. He should leave the rectory in the morning; he had trespassed on this family's hospitality long enough.

At last Charlotte produced the flaming plum pudding and set it down before her father with evident pride. "And here we have the final tradition to complete a right and proper Christmas dinner," she said.

The blue flames slowly flickered out, and everyone clapped.

"What a lovely pudding, my dear," said Mrs. Brigham. "I've never seen a finer."

"Charlotte and her 'proper' Christmas traditions," Eleanor said, rolling her eyes. "That's all she talks about."

"You sneer at me, yet you enjoy the Christmas joy and cheer as much as any," Charlotte snapped back. "Traditions are important; they strengthen our country, and they make Christmas the loveliest holiday of all."

Dan studied Charlotte's flushed cheeks and heard the tension in her voice.

"While traditions surely have their place in a home," he said clearly, "Christmas is the celebration of Christ's birth, and with it His death and resurrection. God's love and sacrifice are what sets this holiday apart."

All eyes turned to Dan. He read varying responses, from scorn to approval.

"There you go, Char. Finally, someone puts you in your place," Clive Brigham said with a chuckle.

"Thank you for this timely reminder, Mr. Jackson," the rector said, smiling. "I'll take a small slice of pudding, my dear, and no sauce."

Charlotte pulled her stunned gaze away from Dan and began to serve her pudding.

Dan accepted a slab of pudding on a china plate but felt too miserable to eat more than a bite or two. He pulled the rest apart with his fork and tried to respond politely to the rector's comments.

"Would you light the candles on the tree?" A voice spoke almost into his ear. He turned to meet Mrs. Colburn's eager gaze and nodded. She led him to the hallway, handed him a lighted taper, and put her finger to her smiling lips.

Dan slipped into the parlor. A fir tree stood on a side table, its branches draped with strings of beads and laden with little gifts. He climbed on a chair to light the top candles, working quickly and cautiously.

What would the Colburns say if he were to admit that this was his first Christmas tree ever? Although this particular tradition was relatively new to England, brought from Germany by Prince Albert, the fashion for Christmas trees had swept throughout Queen Victoria's realm and beyond.

Just after he lighted the last candle, the parlor door burst open and the twins rushed inside. Dan smiled at their exuberance. Together they inspected the gifts hanging from the tree branches while the adults followed at a more sedate pace.

He retreated to a quiet corner to watch the family and friends receive their gifts. Seeing Charlotte's shining eyes as she held up a delicate pair of earbobs and thanked the Brigham family, he felt a twinge of anger at his penniless state.

He could offer her nothing. Nothing at all.

The rector stood in front of the parlor door, blocking Dan's only possible exit. He met Dan's gaze and smiled in his benign way, then approached. "Thank you for taking part. Your presence with us is a great blessing."

"My presence?" Dan said. "I contribute nothing important."

"On the contrary, you contribute much. Your timely reminder that Christmas is the celebration of Christ's birth—"

"I embarrassed her."

"Perhaps, yet the hurt was unintentionally given."

Dan shrugged slightly. "I enjoy beauty, good food, and tradition as much as the next man, but without Christ it all means nothing."

Mr. Colburn thumped Dan's shoulder. "Amen and amen!" He chuckled, then sobered into thoughtfulness. "Charlotte often mistakes the traditions for the truth. She strives to produce Christmas joy by doing everything perfectly, like a holiday version of Martha. True joy can be found only in worshiping at Jesus' feet, like Mary. In a few succinct words, you corrected her error. To my pleased surprise, she accepted the reproof from you without a murmur."

"Only because I am a stranger and a guest," Dan said.

"Hmm. I think not." The rector's smile held a mysterious glint. He moved on to visit with the squire, leaving Dan to wonder.

After the guests departed and the little fir tree

stood dark and empty, Dan and the rector both helped clean up the kitchen. The family members sang as they worked, choosing lively carols at first and closing with "Silent Night."

Dan no longer wished to escape upstairs. He wanted the day to last forever. He wiped dishes and handed them to the girls to put away. Once Charlotte gripped his thumb along with a platter. Did she even notice? He couldn't be sure.

But when at last the work was done, he could think of no excuse to linger. He said his good nights to his host and hostess, and winked and waved at the twins. Eleanor ignored him, but Charlotte met his gaze. She quickly looked away, and his spirits plummeted.

At the base of the stairs, with his hand grasping the newel post, he stopped and stared at the bottom riser. Charlotte should have her own room back. He was no longer ill. Tomorrow he must take leave of this wonderful family and strike out to find work. Somehow he would find a way to pay them back for their hospitality and generosity. As if love could ever be repaid.

"Mr. Jackson, please wait!"

He turned, gripping the post until his knuckles whitened. Candlelight from a wall sconce caught in Charlotte's gleaming curls and glowed upon her skin as she gazed up at him, both hands behind her back. Suddenly shy, she lowered her gaze. "I wanted to thank you—for what you said today—over the pudding. You were right, and as soon as you spoke I knew it. These past weeks I've been trying to manufacture Christmas cheer instead of simply enjoying Christ."

She looked up into his eyes, and a great lump filled Dan's chest. He gave a jerky nod. "Not to say that the greenery and the tree and all weren't beautiful; they were." His voice sounded like iron scraping over gravel. "And the food was delicious. I've never eaten better in my life. God blessed us, every one, as Tiny Tim would say."

She smiled. "I'll never again read that story without thinking of you. The voice you used for Marley's ghost gave me gooseflesh!"

He held her gaze and tried to return the smile.

"I want you to have this." She brought her hands from behind her back and held out a dark lump. When he merely looked down at it, she took hold of his hands and pushed the soft something into his grasp. The touch of her slim fingers shocked him so that he nearly dropped the gift.

"For you." She looked abashed, yet determined.

His hands were shaking so hard that he could scarcely control them. A knitted muffler unrolled from his grasp and dangled nearly to the floor. He caught a pair of mittens just in time.

"They are dark blue, though you cannot tell by candlelight. I thought you—you might like to have them." Suddenly she sounded uncertain, even worried.

"I can think of naught I'd like better," he said firmly. He met her gaze. "I have no gift for you."

Her sudden smile dazzled him. "I'm so thankful you like it! I've wanted to give it to you all day but never found the right time. This is the best part of Christmas." She appeared ready to touch his hands again, but caught herself. "May Jesus fill your heart with great joy, Dan Jackson."

"And you, Miss Charlotte." He had never spoken her name aloud before. It sounded like a caress.

She stepped back, rubbing and twining her hands together, then turned and hurried toward the kitchen. He heard a quiet "Good night" before she vanished.

♪ ♪ ♪

After the house was dark and everyone else had retired to bed for the night, Charlotte sat on the kitchen floor beside an oil lamp turned low and cuddled the kittens. Once roused, they were eager to play and socialize. Her favorite was Humphrey, not only because Dan favored him and had named him, but also because the kitten liked to look into her eyes and pat her nose and cheeks with his soft paws. He seemed aware of her as a person and a friend, not merely as a pair of hands that stroked and played.

Again and again her mind recalled two scenes of the day.

The first scene had played out in Father's study. When she closed her eyes she could picture Clive's amused grin. "Char, you can't mean it. You're like a sister to me; you always have been. I know our mothers talked about us marrying someday, but it was all a game. You're a pretty girl, for certain, but I could never see you—that way. *You* know."

Charlotte buried her nose in the fluff of Humphrey's back and grimaced. The idiot! If she had already known, why would she have questioned his feelings for her?

The second scene: Her encounter with Dan Jackson in the front hall. That memory brought a different kind of heat into her face and body. His mysterious dark eyes, the attractive lines of his face when he smiled, his rough hands trembling in her grasp, his deep voice speaking her name. Oh yes, he found her attractive. A selfish part of her heart exulted in Dan's admiration, the same part that resented Clive's immunity to her charms.

However, Dan Jackson was not only of a social class several steps below Charlotte's, he was also destitute—without a penny to his name. Why had she flirted with him? Why, when she touched his hands, had she felt that shock of attraction? She was no siren, deliberately enticing a man she could never consider taking as a beau. The danger, the hazard of luring a man, then spurning him—such things had never thrilled her before.

And they did not thrill her now. Shame burned a path up her throat and emerged in a sob. A loving relationship with a man she could respect and adore—that was her heart's desire. Wasn't it?

A tear burned a path down her cheek. She wiped it away with Humphrey's soft head. He purred.

Chapter 6

On Boxing Day morning, Dan rose early, washed, and shaved. Staring out the window, he imagined Charlotte as his wife, seated behind him at the dressing table, brushing out her shining hair. A wave of longing for a home and family of his own flowed over him until he nearly drowned in it.

Ice rimed the windowpanes. Cold filtered through the cracks around the frame. Below lay the winter-dead garden, its gate, and the path leading to the church. Beyond the church ran the north-south highway. His hands clenched in dread. Soon he would walk that lonely road once more, never to see this house, this family—Charlotte—again.

Slowly he turned away from the window and left the

room that had been his haven for eight days. His tread upon the stairs was equally slow. Clutching the newel post at the base, he pictured Charlotte and felt again the grasp of her hands on his.

"You're not planning to leave us, I hope."

Dan lifted his gaze to see the rector standing in his study doorway. "I am, sir."

"On Boxing Day? You'll not find work today, my lad. Wait a few days and see what the Lord brings."

Looking into the rector's kindly eyes, Dan recognized genuine affection. "You truly wish me to stay? But why?"

"There would be a great outcry if you were to disappear this morning. I believe a few hearts might quietly break. I believe mine might be among them. I had greatly counted on training and teaching you. So seldom do I find a student willing to subject himself voluntarily to my lectures."

Dan smiled at the jest. "But I cannot live on your charity when I am well and strong."

"I dare say you've not yet regained your full strength. Which brings to mind—I mentioned your work experience to the squire yesterday. He needs a good man in his stables. The beginning position and salary would be small, but there is great potential for future advancement." He beckoned. "Come into my study, have a muffin, and discuss business. I insist."

♪ ♪ ♪

As soon as Charlotte stepped into the upper hallway that morning her gaze fell upon the open door to her bedroom. She rushed to look inside and saw no evidence that Dan Jackson had ever inhabited it.

She clattered down the stairs and rushed to the kitchen. Startled kittens scampered behind the stove. Molly dropped a wooden spoon on the flagstone floor and clutched at her chest. "Miss Charlotte, how you frightened me!"

"Has he gone?"

"Has who gone? The rector?"

"Mr. Jackson."

"Not that I seen, miss. He and the rector was holed up talking in the study when I got 'ere and built the fires. Did you have a nice Christmas, Miss Charlotte?" She picked up the spoon, almost returned it to the porridge pot, then thought better of it, and selected a clean one.

Recalling her lost manners, Charlotte smiled. "We had a lovely holiday, Molly. How is your family? Happy Boxing Day to you."

Three little heads appeared from beneath the stove

and the china dresser. Seeing no cat-starved monsters, the kittens dashed back out to play. Harvey leaped after Molly's apron strings and fell on his face.

Molly tried to ignore him. "Thank you, miss. My family is thriving right well. My sister, what ailed over summer, has picked up some color and fat on her."

"I'm so pleased to hear it, Molly." Thinking of the lace cuffs waiting in Molly's gift box, Charlotte smiled again. Her mother would give Molly her Boxing Day gifts later in the morning. "So Mr. Jackson and the rector are in the study?"

"They was last I seen."

"Thank you."

Humphrey rubbed about Charlotte's ankles, hidden beneath her petticoats. She scooped him up and held his soft purring body to her cheek, then draped him over her shoulder. He flopped there like a tiny scarf with his legs and tail dangling. She placed one hand on his back, but he seemed secure enough.

On a whim, she headed toward the study and knocked at the closed door.

"Enter," her father said.

He and Mr. Jackson were seated at the desk, bending over open books. Mr. Jackson appeared to be taking notes. He looked up, and his quill tipped sideways, blotting ink across the page. Both men rose to their feet.

"Good morning, my dear," her father said, beaming with satisfaction. "As you see, Mr. Jackson and I have begun our theological studies. We have come to an agreement. Although I have offered to teach him simply for the pleasure it will provide me, he insists upon paying for the instruction and finding separate lodgings."

"But where will you stay?" Charlotte asked, gazing into Mr. Jackson's eyes. "And where will you work?"

He opened his mouth, but Father spoke first. "The Lord will supply. For the present, he will sleep over the kitchen in the empty servants' quarters."

Charlotte nodded, trying to think of an intelligent comment. She smiled and bobbed a curtsey. Humphrey chose that moment to jump down from her shoulder. She grasped at him, but he used her bouffant skirts as a safety net, slid down, and hopped to the carpet. With a chirping *mew* and fur standing on end, he scuttled under the sofa.

"What prompted that display, I wonder?" Charlotte said, smoothing the snags caused by tiny claws in her gray wool gown.

"A sudden burst of kitty high spirits, I reckon." Mr.

Jackson went down on his hands and knees to peer beneath the sofa. "Humphrey—here, kitty, kitty."

Charlotte knelt beside him, pushing aside her ballooning skirts. "I don't see him. Where did he go?"

Mr. Jackson tipped his face toward her. "Exploring." His tone held a hint of thrills and adventure.

She met his gaze and grinned.

Charlotte found it difficult now to imagine her life without Dan Jackson in it.

♪ ♪ ♪

The following week passed quickly for Dan. Whenever he considered applying for a position at Brigham Grange, the thought of working for young Clive galled—so he waited. His life of study fell into a pattern that seldom linked with Charlotte's social plans, yet he usually glimpsed her several times during the day, and she seemed to enjoy conversing with him. It would be pure foolishness to imagine that she found him attractive. He was well aware that Clive Brigham held Charlotte's heart; although, he was equally aware that Master Clive regarded her affection with slightly amused, slightly irritated indifference.

One afternoon, his head so full of information that it began to ache, Dan finally closed the theology books and replaced them on their proper shelves. The timeline of Old Testament patriarchs, judges, kings, and prophets enthralled him, though he saw more practical use in the study of God's attributes. So much to learn!

Rubbing his temple with one hand, he closed the study door behind himself. It must be nearly time to dress for dinner. Not that he had fine clothes to change into—his version of dressing was a quick wash and comb. His first purchase, when he did find work, would be a decent suit of clothes and new boots.

"Mr. Jackson."

He looked up to see Charlotte descending the stairs. She looked exceptionally lovely. His face must have revealed his thoughts, for she smiled shyly. "I am attending a charades party at Brigham Grange tonight. Would you like to join us? It is not a formal occasion— Clive didn't even send invitations."

"I think not."

"I wish you would." She reached the bottom step and stood there, her eyes level with his. "The party will be more fun if you come." He caught himself looking at her mouth as she spoke. Quickly he averted his gaze to the wall.

"I haven't proper clothes for a party."

"I don't care what you wear."

Did she have any idea how she affected him? Whenever she spoke with him, he forgot his low social status and his doubtful future. Whenever she spoke with him, he felt like a man whose world held no limits—in fact, like a man who could *conquer* worlds!

"I—I can't. If you'll please excuse me. . ." He bowed slightly and headed toward the kitchen.

Once in his garret chamber, he went to his knees beside the bed and held his head with both hands. "Lord God, help me!"

♪ ♪ ♪

Disappointment rippled through Charlotte, and her anticipation of the party faded. Clive would treat her like a younger sister. Some of the village boys would flirt with her and flatter her, but they would mean nothing by it.

She should just stay home. Perhaps Dan would read to her beside the fire again. They could play with the kittens and talk, and he would catch her gaze and hold it until her heart filled her chest.

But no matter how much she enjoyed Dan's companionship, there was no avoiding the fact that their paths would soon diverge. He would do the Lord's work in a big city, preaching and evangelizing among the poor.

She would marry Clive or some other dull, well-to-do, middle-class fellow, settle down in a drafty barn of a house, raise a brood of children, and grow bored and fat and melancholy.

Gloom settled over her spirit like a mist on the moors.

Chapter 7

D an puffed out a breath and watched it dissipate against the dark backdrop of the church tower. His boots crunched in a light fall of snow. The eve of a new year had arrived, and he felt no closer to a solution to his problems. The temptation to accept Mr. Colburn's offer of scriptural training as a gift tormented him night and day, almost as often as the temptation to remain near. . .

Charlotte. She seemed to like him well enough; they conversed easily, and she listened with interest while he spoke of his missionary calling. At times he recognized a singular light in her eyes when she met his gaze—but he could easily be mistaken. He was no expert on women and their ways.

Again he sighed deeply and coughed. The cold air bit at his face and fingers but no longer ached in his lungs. He felt strong, well fed, healthy—ready to work, if any work could be found.

Lord God, I don't know what to do or where to go. I can't accept charity schooling and be a burden on the rector; a man must carry his own weight. But the opportunity to learn and study Your Word—how can I pass it by? Guide my steps, Lord. I am at a loss.

The sound of scraping caught his attention. Circling the church building, he saw a large and well-bundled figure shoveling snow from the church walkway. "Joe?" Not loud enough. Moving closer, he called again. "Joe!"

Joe paused and looked over his shoulder. "Aye, man? How can I be helping? If you're needin' the rector, he'll be in his study at the—" He paused and frowned. "Do I know ye?"

"I'm the man you found sleeping on the pew and took to the rectory."

Joe's wrinkled brow cleared. "And so y' are. Recovered your sleep, I see. Fine people, them Colburns. The good Lord sets store by them such people. Always looking out for others, they be. Summat troubling ye, lad?"

Dan brushed snow from a marble headstone and decided to unload his burdens. "I need work. The rector has offered to train me in the scriptures—has already started educating me so I can return home and preach—but while I'm training I need work and lodging. I can't live any longer off the minister's bounty. He's been generous—they've treated me like family—but if I stay longer I'll feel like a tick on a dog, sucking it dry."

Joe rested his enormous hands on the shovel's handle and frowned in concentration. "Ye might ask at the Red Stag, or maybe at The Bell in Culverton, up the road a piece. Or Mr. Brigham might take on a gamekeeper or groom."

Dan straightened his shoulders. "I'll try the first two, but I can't see myself working for—for the squire. I can't help believing that God must have something else in mind."

"You keep believing, lad." A smile gleamed through Joe's bushy beard. "You keep right on believing."

"Thank you for the help." Dan started off, then stopped at the end of the walkway and turned back. "Thank you also for helping me that night—" He blinked. How could a man Joe's size vanish that quickly? He must have ducked inside the church. Dan shook his head in wonder. The walkway was neatly shoveled and swept, ready for the end-of-year worship service that night.

Dan headed into town. Houses and shops jutted into the narrow road through Little Brigham, scarcely leaving room for a carriage to pass. Just this side of the market square, Dan saw the sign of the Red Stag hanging above the door of a gabled, half-timbered building. Beyond the inn, an arched-stone gateway in a block wall undoubtedly conducted travelers to the stables behind the inn.

The public room held a few customers—travelers, judging by their appearance. The stout woman wiping out tankards behind the bar gave Dan a short look. "Fresh out o' shepherd's pie," she said.

"I'm looking for the innkeeper, ma'am," Dan said, doffing his cap.

She rested her forearms on the counter and spoke gruffly though not unkindly. "He's around back at the stable, but I wouldn't bother 'im iffen I was you. He be in a right foul mood, him." She laughed without humor, then squinted her eyes and gave Dan an assessing look. "You'd be that drifter what the rector took in. Come to think on it, you might be in luck if you're looking for work."

"I am."

She sniffed. "I 'eard you was sickly. You don't looks it. Do you know 'orses?"

"I do."

A smile transformed her face into cherubic sweetness. "Tell Mister Cuttlesworth that the missus sent you round. Go on with you now." She swept her towel at him. "Through that door and on back."

Encouraged, Dan searched until he located a short, stout man harnessing a pair of grays to a fine brougham. "Mr. Cuttlesworth?"

"That be my name. Don't bother me; I'm right busy. Gentry passing through, wanting fresh 'osses and that fast."

"Yes, sir." Dan stepped forward to hold one of the skittish horses steady enough for Mr. Cuttlesworth to hitch it to the carriage. "Easy there, lad," he soothed. The horse stopped tossing its head and sniffed Dan's breath, its nostrils fluttering. "Aye, you smell the mint I chewed." Dan grinned.

He ran his fingers over the animals' headstalls and blinders, settled the collars more comfortably over their shoulders, and checked their legs for swelling. He looked up to see Mr. Cuttlesworth observing him through narrowed eyes.

"You knows 'osses then?"

Dan nodded. "Worked as 'ostler at the Lion & Unicorn in Birmingham before the war. Tended cavalry mounts and gun mules in the Crimea. I'm seeking a job.

Mrs. Cuttlesworth sent me to find you."

"What's your name?"

Dan told him. "The sexton, Joe, sent me here to ask about work."

"Never 'eard of him. You living in town?"

"I've been lodging with the rector, but I need a room."

"We got better than a room. The 'ostler here gets the cottage at the end of the stable block—or he did 'til he run off last night with the haberdasher's wife. Let's see what you can do, lad."

A short time later, Dan drove the team to the front of the inn. A fine gentleman and his lady emerged from the inn's double doors and mounted their carriage. "Thank you, my good man," the gentleman said and flipped Dan a shilling.

Dan returned to the stable and located the exhausted job horses that had needed replacing. Mr. Cuttlesworth had thrown a blanket over each of the beasts, but they were both still sweating and shaking. Dan led the geldings around the yard until they cooled; then he prepared bran mash, warming it on the cast-iron stove in the tack room. The animals ate gratefully, then dozed and nibbled at hay while he brushed dried sweat and mud from their shaggy winter coats. Only afterward did Dan let them drink and put them away for a well-earned rest.

After cleaning up the tack room, splicing a broken bridle, and rinsing out some soiled blankets, he brushed off his hands and wondered whether or not Mr. Cuttlesworth intended to hire him. He nearly ran into the innkeeper as he stepped into the passageway. Mr. Cuttlesworth lifted his lamp.

"You been 'ere three hours, and the place looks like new. You're hired, Jackson."

Dan walked back to the rectory late that night, carrying a package under one arm and softly whistling "God Rest Ye Merry, Gentlemen."

Charlotte met him at the door. "There you are! We were growing worried."

"I sent a message boy." He pulled off his cap as he stepped inside.

"That was hours ago. But, Dan, I'm so pleased you found work! You'll still live here, of course." She took his cap and hung it on a hook, then unwrapped the muffler from his neck.

"Nay, I've a cottage of my own. Four rooms and a loft. I'll soon set it to rights." He could smell himself—sweat, dust, and horses. "I'm in need of a wash."

"Come to the scullery and wash up for a late supper.

Soon we shall all walk over to church for the New Year sing and prayers."

He obediently followed her through the house, trying not to watch her too blatantly. In a plum-colored gown of shiny-striped fabric, she looked too pretty for words. She set her lamp on the scullery table, tied on an apron, poured water into a basin for him, then laid out clean toweling. "The water was scalding just minutes ago. It should be comfortably warm now. I'll prepare a plate while you wash."

"Thank you." He wondered where the other family members might be hiding. This being alone with Charlotte felt too right, almost as if they were husband and wife in their own cottage.

She lighted a candle from the lamp, set it in a holder, and left him alone in the scullery. Her candlelight faded into darkness. Dan stripped off his soiled jacket and shirt, plunged his hands into the warm water, and began to scrub his upper body and head.

While he was toweling off, Humphrey wandered into the scullery and mewed in greeting. For such a tiny beast, the cat had a lot of awareness and personality. Dan bent over to pick him up. Humphrey purred and kneaded his shoulder.

"Mr. Jackson, my father found garments for you."

Charlotte's voice indicated her approach. "They're from the missionary barrel and far from new, but we thought you might like another change of clothing. Especially now that you have a—"

"Miss Charlotte," Dan called, "unless you wish to see a man without a shirt, you'd best come no farther!" He had little patience with modern women and their ridiculous sensibilities, yet neither did he wish to shock or embarrass the girl. "I purchased new garments today."

A pause. "Oh," she squeaked. "Very well." He heard her skirts rustle as she retreated.

She wasn't in the kitchen when he passed through it on his way to the tiny staircase leading to the servants' quarters. He shook his head and smiled ruefully. How would a lady like Charlotte survive in the crowded slums of Birmingham, where people often dispensed with their outer garments on hot summer days? Could she adapt and accept people for who they were instead of judging them by their attire? Or would she wither away like a rose plucked from its garden? He would never know, of course.

In his bedchamber, he unwrapped his parcel. When had he last owned new clothes? He changed into clean cotton drawers and a starched white shirt. Never owned a white shirt before. The suit seemed well made, though its fabric was rather coarse. The jacket's fit was tight across the shoulders, but otherwise the garments were adequate. He knotted his tie beneath his chin and tucked it into the waistcoat.

"Your supper is ready, Mr. Jackson!" Charlotte called from below.

Was it his imagination, or did her voice betray a quiver of anticipation? He ran the comb through his shaggy hair one last time, straightened his shoulders, and descended the creaky stairs into the kitchen.

She stood before the china dresser with her hands clasped at her waist. The kittens frolicked around her skirts. Her gaze inspected Dan from head to new boots. "You look very fine," she said at last.

"Fancy feathers," he commented. "Hope I tied the neckcloth right."

She approached him slowly, her eyes on his necktie, and reached to straighten it. He swallowed hard. "Didn't you have one on your army uniform?" she asked.

"Not like this."

"You must have looked handsome in uniform." She gave the tie a final pat, and he thought he might fall over backward.

While he ate cold pork pie, rye bread, and boiled cabbage, she settled across the table from him. "My father tells me you are learning quickly."

Dan was careful to keep his mouth closed while he chewed.

She continued. "Now that you have work, how can you continue your studies?"

He swallowed. "I'll find time. A man makes time for things that are important to him."

"So you'll still come to the rectory? For studies, I mean?" She lowered her gaze to her clasped hands. "I hope you'll dine with us occasionally, too."

A stinging pain in his leg distracted his attention. "Oww!" Humphrey climbed his trouser leg like a tree and hopped into his lap. "You little beast!" Dan couldn't help grinning as the kitten poked its face over the table-top and batted at the cabbage with one white paw.

"Humphrey!" Charlotte cried. "These kittens are becoming spoiled beyond imagining. The twins allow them too much license."

"I've scarcely seen the twins lately."

"They spend much time at their cousins' house, and you've been lost in your world of books." Charlotte rose and circled the table. "Do you want me to take him away?"

What he wanted was to wrap his arm around her and draw her close. "No, I don't mind him."

The front door closed, and voices filtered through to the kitchen. Charlotte hurriedly moved away. "Mother and the girls are back. Father is already at the church."

It suddenly dawned on Dan that he and Charlotte had been alone in the rectory all this time, chaperoned only by three kittens. He suddenly felt short of breath.

♪ ♪ ♪

Charlotte stood between her mother and Priscilla, trying to listen to her father's sermon. Despite her best efforts, her mind kept wandering. Since she first became fully aware of Clive, years ago, she had never noticed any other boy or man. All her plans had focused on him, all her efforts went into attracting his notice, all her dreams of the future took place inside his hereditary home, Brigham Grange.

Until Dan Jackson swept into her life. Each encounter with him was more exciting than the last. According to her father, Dan had an exceptional mind, a remarkable understanding of theological mysteries, and a close relationship with the Lord Himself. He was a man who would love his wife and lead his family in godly ways—a man much like her father, for all their external differences.

Adding to his appeal was the fact that Charlotte

felt more attractive and more of a woman in his presence than with any other man of her acquaintance. This might be the result of his obvious admiration, but Charlotte thought not. Between them lay a strong and mysterious bond.

Could it be that God intended Charlotte to exchange her grand dreams for a short, hard, sacrificial life in a drafty shack in the big city? No! She gave her head a sharp shake. God knew better than to ask such a thing.

Mother looked over at her in surprise. Charlotte tried to smile reassuringly. But then she caught Dan's quick glance over Priscilla's head, and her heart leaped. Why did he have to be so attractive? Life with him would bring nothing but hardship and pain.

The New Year peal of bells rang out from the church tower.

Chapter 8

Dan forked manure and soiled bedding into the dung cart, then wheeled it to the refuse heap in the inn's courtyard. Steam rose from both the cart and his body as soon as he stepped outside.

While he worked, his mind dwelt on intriguing topics. The infinity and omnipotence of God, the inerrancy of scripture, the question of free will versus predestination—he loved it all. The joy he found in discussing and debating such topics with the reverend Mr. Colburn had taken him by surprise. Who would have thought that a latent theologian could dwell in the form of a humble hostler? Who would have thought that opportunity to study such holy topics would ever come the way of Dan Jackson?

He smiled while dumping the cart. Gratitude toward

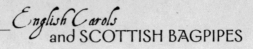

God put lightness in his steps and strength in his body even as he performed the most mundane of chores.

"Mr. Jackson?"

Drusilla and Priscilla Colburn trotted across the brick courtyard. Bundled in warm clothing until they each appeared twice normal size, they beamed at the sight of him, big eyes glowing in their pointed little faces.

"Good morning, ladies. What brings you here? Where's your mother?" He brushed his grimy hands down his trouser legs. Despite the cold, he worked in his shirtsleeves.

"Mother let us come to town with Charlotte and Eleanor, who are shopping for fripperies. Tonight is the big Twelfth Night party, you know."

"That it is."

"Just now we saw Millicent Brigham carrying an enormous wreath. The hall at the Red Stag will be glorious!" Drusilla sighed and clasped her mittened hands beneath her chin.

"You're coming, aren't you?" asked Priscilla. "We want to dance with you."

Dan smiled at her blunt pronouncement. "You honor me, ladies; but nay, short of a miracle, I'll not be attending the party."

"But why not?" Priscilla said. "You live right here at the inn."

"I'll be doing my job, that's why not. All the people traveling to town for the party will need someone to care for their horses. That someone would be me." Dan kept his tone light and tipped his cap. "Now, if you'll be excusing me, I must attend to my labors."

The girls followed him back into the stable. " 'Tis most unfair," Drusilla insisted. "You should have your chance at fun like everyone else. Couldn't you get the horses settled, then come to the party for even a short time?"

"Mr. Cuttlesworth hired me to do this job. I'll not be leaving the stable until every last guest has departed for home. That's the way of it, little friends. I'm a working-man, not a gentleman." He smiled at the girls to remove any sting from his words, then picked up his pitchfork and shifted another load of muck into the cart.

Priscilla frowned, and Drusilla looked ready to cry. Both girls walked along the row of stalls, inspecting the backsides of the resident horses. "You need Humphrey to come live with you," Priscilla said, "as soon as he's grown. I just saw a mouse."

"There are mice enough here to keep a dozen cats employed," Dan said, grateful for the change in subject.

"Charlotte will be sad that you're not coming to-night." Drusilla refused to be distracted. "She likes you as much as we do."

"I don't know that she does anymore," Priscilla said. "She gets all red and irritated when we talk about him much, and she drops things."

Feeling red and irritated himself, Dan tried not to hear the girls' chatter.

"Yesterday she cried all over Humphrey. His fur was wet and gloppy."

"But she might not be crying about Dan. She's been dismal all week and talks only to Father in his study," Priscilla said. "Can you picture Char living here?" She waved her hand to indicate the stable and its environs. "She might like Dan extremely, but she'd never marry an 'ostler. She wants to be lady of the manor."

Keeping his face averted, Dan grimaced. Trust Priscilla to summarize the entire matter in a few concise words. He paused to draw his sleeve across his forehead and his suddenly burning eyes.

♪ ♪ ♪

Charlotte regarded her reflection in the blotchy, wavy mirror. Glossy curls framed her sober face. Noticing the pronounced droop to her lips, she attempted a smile and immediately felt tears spring to her eyes. Annoyed, she turned away from the mirror and smoothed her long gloves.

Other young ladies clustered behind her in the small space, smoothing their hair and arranging their necklines to show as much of their shoulders as they dared. Charlotte felt lost in a sea of rustling, colliding skirts. Excited chatter assaulted her ears.

What had become of her joy in the season? Laces and ribbons and silks no longer satisfied her desires. The prospect of dancing with Clive left her heart unmoved by either dread or happiness. The Twelfth Night party, anticipated for months, now loomed before her as a trial to be endured.

Despite a cold wind, the Colburn family had walked to the inn from the rectory. Pattens protected the girls' dancing slippers, and frozen mud could not soil their skirts. Father saw no reason to hire a carriage when they could easily walk the distance.

So the girls had found no excuse to visit the inn's stables. Dan was undoubtedly too busy for conversation anyway. Charlotte would only be in his way.

She returned to the ballroom and observed her surroundings with a sense of detachment. A new certainty awakened in her heart, spreading warmth throughout her body. Closing her eyes, she pressed her hands to her hot cheeks and recognized the truth.

A lifetime of poverty and hardship with Dan would

be preferable to splendor and comfort without him.

♪ ♪ ♪

Dan barked orders to a stable boy hired to assist him for the evening. A pair of dapple grays hitched near the pump whinnied, and the squire's handsome Cleveland bays answered with ringing neighs that echoed through the courtyard. Dan heard a snatch of orchestra music before another carriage rattled into the yard.

Many drivers left their horses hitched in the court-yard or street, gave them nosebags, and covered them with blankets for the duration of the party. Dan had actually stabled only the few beasts belonging to those responsible for setting up the party. He glanced up at the inn and shivered.

"Why ain't you a-dancin' at yon party, lad?"

The deep, gruff voice startled Dan out of his rev-erie. "Eh?"

"A young buck oughtn't to be cooling 'is 'eels in the stableyard whilst pretty ladies be without partners inside." Joe, the sexton, tipped his shaggy head toward the inn. "Why not step inside for an hour and tramp the boards? I kin 'andle things out here for ye."

Dan shook his head. "Thank you, but Mr. Cuttles-worth wouldn't take to that. He hired me to do the job."

He tilted his head and gave the hulking giant a closer look. "Why do I never see you about town?"

Joe's teeth flashed in a beam of lamplight. "Turn about, how's come I seldom see *you*, lad? I reckon you and me walks different paths. But ye needn't try to shift the subject. I know for a fact that Mr. Cuttlesworth wouldn't object to ye leaving the 'osses to my keeping for an hour. Ask 'im yourself, if ye can't be taking my word on it."

An overwhelming desire to make the attempt caught Dan by surprise. His entire body shook, and not with cold. He glanced down at himself. By the time he washed and changed—

"Clothes be 'anged. It's you the lady wants to see."

Dan's rational mind rejected the plan, yet his heart wanted to heed Joe's advice. "But Mr. Cutt—"

" 'Ere be the man 'isself. Ask 'im."

Joe faded into the shadows as Mr. Cuttlesworth approached. "Dan, you're a wonder, a fair wonder. I never seen the like!" He glanced around the courtyard at the quiet, contented horses, the few drivers conversing or dozing on their boxes, the starlit sky above. "The Bethlehem stable could ha' been no more peaceful!"

"If I might ask, sir, would you take kindly to my stepping inside for a time? I'd greatly care to dance one or two dances, and Joe the sexton offers to watch things here for me—"

Mr. Cuttlesworth waved his hand airily. "If ever I met a lad deserving of his chance at happiness, it's you. Only mind you're back afore the rush."

Dan closed his gaping mouth, blinked twice, and nodded. "Certainly, sir."

Mr. Cuttlesworth trotted on back to the inn. Joe reappeared at Dan's elbow. "Best wash up quick-like and find your young lady. She'll be pining for ye."

As if in a dream, Dan hurried to his cottage, washed, shaved, and changed into his good clothes. Dark hair hung almost into his eyes and waved on the back of his neck. Fine clothes didn't change his nature, but no matter. If Charlotte couldn't accept him for his true self, her regard would be worthless.

Doubt assailed him as soon as he stepped into the hall. Greenery, ribbons, candles, and strings of beads adorned the walls, and large kissing balls hung above every arch. He saw one laughing young woman ducking in and out of an archway while her persistent suitor endeavored to catch her beneath the ball.

Dan searched the crowd for a familiar face. There was Charlotte on the dance floor, performing some kind of country dance opposite Clive Brigham. He was talking to her with animation, but she seemed strangely apathetic, lacking her usual sparkle. Nevertheless, her beauty built a lump in Dan's chest until he could scarcely breathe.

What had he been thinking? Why would a woman like that want to dance with him? He prowled the edges of the throng, overhearing snatches of conversation, dodging a running child.

"Dan!" The twins emerged from a group of children in one corner.

Priscilla nearly tackled him in an exuberant hug. "You came! I knew you would come. Has Charlotte seen you?"

"No."

"She's been in the Slough of Despond all evening, just because you weren't here."

He lowered his brows in disbelief. "Did she say that?"

Drusilla joined them, hands folded decorously at her waist. "She never said so, but Mother chided her for sulking. Mother said something else that might have been interesting, but she said it too low for us to hear."

"And then Charlotte got very quiet. She has danced every dance, but she doesn't talk much," Priscilla added, tugging at his arm. "You must ask her for the next dance or she may never be happy again."

The exaggeration lightened Dan's spirits for only a

moment. "I don't know many dances."

"Can you waltz? Most of the dances are waltzes."

"I can waltz—well enough." Not so well, but he should be able to avoid treading on Charlotte's feet.

"Then get ready and go ask her! They finished the set."

As Clive escorted Charlotte from the dance floor, Dan squared his shoulders, coughed, and stepped forward. "Miss Charlotte."

She glanced his way, her eyes widened, and she stopped short. "Dan!"

Another young man moved in to address her. "Miss Charlotte, may I—"

She brushed past him without heed and reached to take Dan's hand. "However did you get away? Father said you must be terribly busy tonight and I shouldn't expect to see you."

"Joe offered to spell me for a time. I—I—Will you dance with me?"

Her face turned pink. "I shall be honored to dance with you, Mr. Jackson."

The orchestra struck the first few notes of a waltz, and Charlotte led Dan to the floor. His boots suddenly felt two sizes too large, and sweat broke out on his forehead. Charlotte placed her hand on his shoulder. He gently laid his callused hand on her little waist, clutched her other hand, and swallowed hard. Would he even be able to move his feet?

♪ ♪ ♪

Charlotte followed her partner's competent lead, amazed at how light he was on his feet. He never stepped near her slippers. They floated over the floor, and her skirt bobbed and swayed to the rhythm.

"Will it suffice?"

She blinked. "Will what suffice?"

"My face. You've stared at it these five minutes without speaking a word. I hoped you might have come to a conclusion." He smiled. "I find yours most pleasing to behold."

"You must know how handsome you are," she said faintly. "I imagine many women have told you so."

His eyes widened. "But for my grandmother, you are the first."

"Surely not!" She slid her hand higher on his shoulder, then back into its proper position. "How old are you?"

"Twenty-four."

The orchestra concluded the waltz with an instrumental flourish, and the dancers slowly emptied the floor. "Dance with me again?" Charlotte asked, then blushed at her own boldness.

"I'll dance with no other," he said quietly, standing close. Somewhere within the folds of her skirt, he still held her hand. Charlotte moved her fingers, and he linked his through them.

People brushed past on both sides, but she paid them no heed. Dan held her full attention. What was he thinking as he gazed so deeply into her eyes? Dared she hope he might ask her father for her hand? But what real use would she be to him in his ministry, a spoiled country girl?

I could do it, Dan. She gently squeezed his hand and leaned closer. *I could make any shack into a home, and I would love my life if you were always in it. Dear God, please let him love me!*

The strength of her longing caught her by surprise. For Dan she would do anything, give anything, only to have him near.

Now his gaze questioned her as if to inquire: *But would your affection last through fire and ice and deprivation? Could you, a delicate flower, thrive in my chosen field?*

"I am strong, Dan. I survived many childhood illnesses, and I can work hard." She spoke her thoughts aloud.

He answered in kind. "It would be harder than you think."

"I enjoy a challenge."

His expression softened. "I know. You're a stubborn little creature."

Strong hands caught them both by the arms and shoved them two steps to one side. Startled and angry, Charlotte tried to jerk out of Clive's grasp, but he laughed and pointed up. "Now you're in the right spot. Kiss her, Jackson! She wants you to."

Dan looked up at the mistletoe kissing ball, then lowered his gaze and sought Charlotte's. She smiled and gave him a tiny nod. To the cheers of a surrounding crowd, Dan kissed her gently. At the touch of his lips on hers, Charlotte lost all doubt.

"Pick a berry, Dan," Eleanor said, laughing and bright for once. "One berry for every kiss."

He reached up to pluck a mistletoe berry from the ball, but two fell into his hand. "I best pay for that with another kiss," he said. This time Charlotte rose on her toes and kissed him back.

Whistles and cheers rewarded them.

Charlotte pulled Dan's head down and spoke into his ear. "Now this is truly a right, proper Christmas— the most joyful ever—because God planned it for us."

Chapter 9

Dan stepped back to admire his handiwork. A coat of whitewash brightened the humble cottage until it fairly sparkled in the spring sunshine. Mrs. Colburn's and Charlotte's hard work in the garden, planting shrubs and roses and flowers, also gave it the look of home. A honeymoon cottage, he thought with an irrepressible smile.

No longer drafty, free of mice thanks to Humphrey, brightened by colorful blooms, and furnished with an assortment of pieces donated by Charlotte's relatives and the Cuttlesworths, the cottage filled its position alongside the inn's stables with pride.

Throughout the winter and well into spring, the rector had taught Dan and counseled the young couple.

Their courtship had progressed largely under the watchful eye of Mrs. Colburn.

Dan intended to continue his scriptural training for at least another year before he and Charlotte moved to Birmingham. He wanted to purchase a comfortable house in the city for his wife, which meant he must continue to work and save every penny. Already he owned a dogcart and a venerable, but healthy, Cleveland bay gelding. Charlotte loved to drive the modest vehicle on country picnics with Dan and her sisters.

The young couple would probably always be obliged to economize, but Dan had long since realized that his fiancée thrived in challenging circumstances. God had provided him with the ideal missionary's wife.

"So the wedding be this night, eh?"

Recognizing that deep voice, Dan slowly turned. "Joe?"

The burly giant grinned affably. "Reckon 'twere Providence brought ye to town that winter's night?"

"I know He did. And He prompted you to send me to the rectory. But, Joe, when did you get back in town? I've mentioned you to several people, including the rector, but no one seems to know you. I had assumed you were sexton at the church, but Charlotte tells me they have none at present."

"I'm here and there, lad. Hither and yon. Ye'll likely not see me again soon, but I'll ne'er forget you and your lovely bride. The Lord will bless ye with long and fruitful years of ministry together. Sorrows, alas, will come, but ye'll carry few regrets. Generations to come will rise up to call ye blessed, and ye'll dandle your grandbabies on your knee."

Dan nodded slowly and removed his cap. "As the Lord wills."

Joe reached over the gate to clap Dan's shoulder with his beefy hand, then walked on down the village street. Dan stared after him. A tingle ran up his spine. Joe turned a corner and was gone.

Feeling pressure on his ankle, Dan looked down. Humphrey twined between his boots. "What are you doing outside, cat? A carriage will run you over, or a dog will swallow you whole."

Humphrey, still a leggy kitten, trotted back to the house and waited for Dan to open the door. "You're right. I'd best wash and dress for the wedding. I'll wear my best suit—black and white like yours."

♪ ♪ ♪

Church bells rang in celebration over Little Brigham. Children frolicked and shouted in the streets as the wedding party streamed from the church doors. Charlotte clung to her new husband's arm beneath a shower of flowers.

Eleanor ran up to give her a kiss. "You'll be happy, Char. I know you will."

Priscilla and Drusilla nearly strangled Dan with hugs. He squeezed them both and gave them matching kisses. "I love my little sisters."

The twins transferred their hugs to Charlotte. "You got the best husband ever," Priscilla said with confidence. "Treat him nice."

"And Humphrey, too," Drusilla added. "We'll feed him every day while you're away. But try not to stay away too long!"

Just before the young couple climbed into their waiting carriage, on loan from Mr. Cuttlesworth, Charlotte's parents claimed their share of hugs. "May God bless you richly as you enter His service together," the rector said, wiping tears from his eyes with his thumb.

Charlotte's mother clung to her a moment longer, kissed Dan's cheek, and stepped back to wave.

Dan climbed to his seat, then threw handfuls of coins into the air. Children squealed and pounced, including the twins. Priscilla's piercing cries of triumph rose above the rest.

With a *cluck* and a slap of reins, Dan started the pair off at a trot. Charlotte turned back to wave as the carriage bumped over the road.

"Who is that man?"

Dan glanced at her. "What man?"

"The big, black-bearded man standing on the church porch. He waved to us. I don't believe I've ever seen him before."

Dan turned around and returned the stranger's wave. With a shrug and a smile, he drove on. "I really couldn't say. A well-wisher, I suppose."

Charlotte faced forward and leaned on his shoulder. "*Now* will you tell me where we are headed? I know Father made the plans, but no matter how I pleaded he gave me not one hint."

He shifted the reins to one hand and wrapped his arm around her. "We're headed to a comfortable inn in a quiet little town nestled amongst the hills, where none will find us. Your parents honeymooned there twenty-four years ago. We'll have an entire week to ourselves. How does this please you, my love?"

She replied with a fervent embrace.

ENGLISH SCONES

2 cups unbleached flour
1 tablespoon baking powder
2 tablespoons sugar
½ teaspoon salt
6 tablespoons butter
½ cup milk
½ cup dried cranberries and ½ teaspoon lemon
    extract
(You may subsititue ½ cup raisins and ½ teaspoon
    almond extract)
1 egg, lightly beaten
Sugar

Mix first four ingredients. Cut in butter until mixture resembles cornmeal. Add milk until dough clings together and is a bit sticky—add more milk if necessary, 1 tablespoon at a time. Add desired fruit and extract. Turn the dough on to a floured surface and pat until about 1½ inches thick. Either cut into wedges or use a biscuit cutter to cut circles. Handle as little as possible. Place scones on ungreased cookie sheet—don't allow them to touch each other. Brush with egg, then sprinkle tops with sugar. Bake at 425° for about 15 minutes or until light brown. Serve with preserves or jam and Mock Devonshire Cream

MOCK DEVONSHIRE CREAM

2 tablespoons powdered sugar
1 (8 ounce) package cream cheese, softened
½ cup sour cream

Stir sugar into cream cheese. Fold in sour cream and blend. Makes 1½ cups.

JILL STENGL

Award-winning author Jill Stengl lives in a log home beside a lake in northern Wisconsin with her husband, children, and three spoiled cats. She has written several Heartsong Presents books and Barbour Publishing anthology novellas. Jill particularly enjoys writing stories set in England, since she and her family lived there for seven years while her husband was in the US Air Force. Her daughter, Anne Elisabeth, created the kitten pen-and-ink drawing for "A Right, Proper Christmas."

A Letter to Our Readers

Dear Readers:

In order that we might better contribute to your reading enjoyment, we would appreciate your taking a few minutes to respond to the following questions. When completed, please return to the following: Fiction Editor, Barbour Publishing, Inc., P.O. Box 719, Uhrichsville, OH 44683.

1. Did you enjoy reading *English Carols and Scottish Bagpipes*?
   ❑ Very much—I would like to see more books like this.
   ❑ Moderately—I would have enjoyed it more if _____

   _____

   _____

2. What influenced your decision to purchase this book?
   (Check those that apply.)
   ❑ Cover   ❑ Back cover copy   ❑ Title   ❑ Price
   ❑ Friends   ❑ Publicity   ❑ Other

3. Which story was your favorite?
   ❑ *I Saw Three Ships*
   ❑ *A Right, Proper Christmas*

4. Please check your age range:
   ❑ Under 18   ❑ 18–24   ❑ 25–34
   ❑ 35–45   ❑ 46–55   ❑ Over 55

5. How many hours per week do you read? _____

Name _____

Occupation _____

Address _____

City_____ State _____ Zip _____

E-mail_____